Shadow of Fear

Jane Peart is a prolific author of romantic fiction who lives in Fortuna, California. She is the author of the Orphan Train West series and the International Romance series.

Shadow of Fear

Jane Peart

Fleming H. Revell

A Division of Baker Book House Co
Grand Rapids, Michigan 49516

Published by Fleming H. Revell
a division of Baker Book House Company
P.O. Box 6287, Grand Rapids, MI 49516-6287

Printed in the United States of America

Library of Congress Cataloging-in-Publication Data

Peart, Jane.
    Shadow of fear / Jane Peart.
        p. cm.
    ISBN 0-8007-5597-9 (paper)
    I. Title.
PS3566.E238S53 1996
813'.54—dc20   96-14568

I had to change coaches in London. I stepped down into the bustling stagecoach courtyard. All was noise and confusion. At least three coaches were being readied for travel—their harnesses checked, luggage strapped on top and behind by coach hands. The clatter of horses' hooves on the cobblestones mingled with the voices of dispatchers yelling at the stable boys, drivers shouting out their destinations, passengers calling for porters, porters rattling by with baggage carts and clamoring for people to make way.

The October morning was dark, the chill air dense with fog. Prospective passengers clustered in little groups, their shoulders hunched against the damp. In spite of my merino cape and fur muff, I shivered, though perhaps more from nerves than from actual cold. This was the first time I'd traveled so far and alone. I stood looking about me in utter bewilderment, wondering whom to ask for the information I needed.

I spotted a burly man wearing a battered beaver top hat, a long fringed muffler wrapped about his neck. He was standing near the open door of one of the coaches as he supervised his helper, who was loading luggage on the top. I hurried toward him.

"Please, sir, is this the coach for Meadowmead?"

"It is," he said gruffly.

"And does it stop at Tynley Junction?"

"It does."

"Oh, good." I sighed, digging into my small purse for the ticket I had purchased beforehand.

"You may as well get in," he said, taking my ticket. "We're about to leave."

Although outwardly I managed to keep my demeanor composed, inwardly I was filled with anxiety. I was setting out on a journey fraught with uncertainties, hazardous even, its outcome unknown. My heart beat wildly. The purpose of my journey was cloaked in lies and deception. For a person who held personal integrity in high regard, this weighed uneasily on my conscience.

Once inside the coach, I settled into a corner of the carriage. Thrusting my kid-gloved hands deeply into my squirrel muff, I felt the edges of the envelope containing Nanny Grace's letter, the reason I'd embarked on this uncertain mission.

A flurry of activity outside and the sounds of raised voices attracted my attention. Suddenly the coach door was yanked open, admitting a draft of cold air. The shovel-bonneted head of a sharp-eyed woman poked inside. Her head turned as she made a quick survey of the interior, then it disappeared. Soon the soberly dressed owner of the bonnet reappeared, climbed in, then turned to assist an elegant elderly lady, obviously her mistress, aboard. Swathed in a fur-lavished, claret-colored cape, the elderly lady wore a bonnet that quivered with egret plumes and framed a thin, finely lined, aristocratic face with a high-bridged nose. She called crossly over her shoulder to someone outside, "Now, not another word, Nicholas!"

While, with a great deal of rustling of taffeta, she took her seat opposite me, she continued speaking to the unseen person outside. "I'm not risking an attack of ague by staying another hour in this wretched weather."

Her words were immediately followed by those of a male voice, tinged with irritation. "This is really unnecessary, Aunt Isabel. Another day and the broken axle on *my* carriage will be fixed. You will be able to travel home in comfort, not in a crowded public conveyance."

"I would hardly call this crowded, Nicholas," the lady replied archly, casting a sharp glance over at me. "There is only one other passenger."

A moment later two hatboxes, a wicker hamper, and a leather tea case were handed inside. Then the head of a man, who would have been extraordinarily handsome were it not for the scowl that brought his heavy dark brows together over piercing gray eyes, leaned in. His mouth was grim as he looked around then let his eyes rest on me.

His gaze made a sweeping inventory from the brim of my bonnet to the tips of my boots, making a swift evaluation of his aunt's traveling companion. I felt my cheeks grow hot, blushing under his calculating appraisal. My instinctive reaction was to tuck my feet under my braid-trimmed skirt. Otherwise, no doubt, he would have counted the buttons on my boots.

Indignant at his steady regard, I wanted to show my annoyance. Certainly this was not a gentlemanly thing to do, even though he *was* dressed like a gentleman in an impeccably tailored caped coat of fine tweed with a velvet collar, and leather gloves. As I stared back at him with as cool a look as I could manage, a strange thing happened. I experienced a sudden sense of recognition. Was it possible we had met somewhere before? That seemed unlikely. I certainly would have remembered. His face—with its classic Greek nose, gray-blue eyes the color of a winter sea, firm yet sensitive mouth—was a face that, once seen, could not easily be for-

7

gotten. It was a ridiculous idea, I told myself, yet the feeling of recognition lingered.

Confused, I turned my head away from his riveting eyes to peer out the misty window. I pretended a great interest in the loading of the luggage on top of the stage, being conducted with much loud discussion.

My attention was then demanded by the woman he had called Aunt Isabel. "Well, young lady, as it seems we are to be fellow travelers on this miserable morning, let me introduce myself. I am Lady Bethune. My maid, Thompson. That fierce-looking gentleman is my nephew, Nicholas Seymour."

Forced to acknowledge the introduction, I murmured, "I am Challys Winthrop."

"*Challys!* What an odd name!"

I thought her comment rather rude. However, perhaps a person past sixty, especially one of her class, felt she had leave to say anything that popped into her head. I did not feel compelled to explain that Challys was a proudly inherited Winthrop family name, nor that most of my family and friends called me Lyssa.

I had much else on my mind other than to pay heed to the somewhat arrogant Lady Bethune, born-to-the-purple though she might have been. I had a long journey ahead of me and much to think about. I turned away from the curious gaze of my companion, pretending to study the dreary scene outside the carriage window.

Try as I might, it was almost impossible not to overhear the continued bickering between Lady Bethune and her nephew.

Finally she said, "Enough, Nicholas. I'm settled, and that's the end of it." She added grudgingly, "I'll send a message as soon as I'm safely home."

With a somewhat ungracious good-bye to his elderly relative, he slammed the door, causing the carriage to rock a little. I got the feeling Nicholas Seymour was not used to defeat and did not take it well.

With a great jangling of harnesses, shouts from the driver and the stagecoach station manager, and a few jolting half-starts, we at last got under way. The heavily loaded topside of the carriage caused the body of the stage to sway and groan ominously on its wheels, which brought muted squeals of alarm from Lady Bethune's maid for which she was abruptly reprimanded by her employer.

"Don't be such a ninny, Thompson."

The coach rumbled through the sleeping city streets, cobbles shiny with heavy moisture. Gas lamplights shed a dim, eerie glow on the tall buildings we passed, which loomed over us like dingy, brick canyon walls.

Past the outskirts of London the landscape changed, but still heavily veiled by fog, it was indistinct. I soon became used to the motion of the stage as we were now on country roads beyond the city. The jolting sensation had a certain rhythm. After a while, I noticed a steady purring sound. A quick glance toward the other occupants of the coach revealed they had both slipped into shallow slumber. Lady Bethune's bonnet was knocked askew, giving her a rakish air. Thompson's neck was tilted at what appeared to be an uncomfortable angle, and through her prim mouth, slightly open, soft snorting noises emanated.

With both my traveling companions asleep, I was afforded a bit of privacy. I drew out Nanny Grace's letter and began rereading it.

Nanny Grace had been both my mother's nurse and then my nurse. Actually, having been educated above her station, she had been more than that. When my mother and I had each reached the proper age, Nanny had served as a governess, teaching us our letters and to read and write. I unfolded the page and read again the few terse lines hurriedly written because of the urgency of the message. As I replaced the letter in its envelope, I felt my stomach tighten from anxiety.

But the die had been cast. There was no turning back now. I had no alternative but to proceed with our desperate plan.

I leaned my head back against the seat. Closing my eyes, I let my thoughts wander.

I had never known a father's protection. I was but an infant when my young soldier father was killed. My mother, hardly more than a child herself at seventeen, went to live with her guardian and godmother, Lord and Lady Hazelton, at their country estate, Briarwood Manor, where I grew up.

As the only child in a household of adults, I was pampered, my every need anticipated, any wish happily granted.

My earliest memories were of my pretty mother, with her golden-brown curls, her sparkling sapphire eyes, her low sweet voice and musical laughter, the feeling with which she would read Bible stories, teaching me even at an early age to trust God. I remember Nanny's warm comforting presence, nursery teas and glowing hearth fires and bedtime stories, the Hazeltons hovering over us with affectionate indulgence, that beautiful house with its polished floors, shining windows, filled, it always seemed, with light, luxury, and love.

My childhood was, as I recall it, a completely happy one until I was twelve, when my mother remarried.

I did not like Henry Muir the first time I met him. I believe I could sense his aversion to children. Of course, at that first encounter, I had no idea my young, unsophisticated mother was planning to marry him.

I had been playing in the garden, Nanny seated on one of the iron lace benches nearby, knitting, when Mama came outside with a tall, dark-haired man.

"Darling, I want you to meet a very special friend of mine, Mr. Muir," Mama announced, a happy lilt in her voice.

My Irish wolfhound's deep-throated growl at Mr. Muir's approach should have warned me further, since animals often seem to have an instinctive awareness of evil. Ran had been my father's dog and so was especially beloved by my mother. At my birth, he became my loving protector and guardian. Now, he pushed his great bulk between me and my mother's companion. My mother did not seem to notice; she was gazing up adoringly at Henry Muir.

"So this is little Challys," a deep voice said.

I looked up from where I had been making a miniature garden, into a pair of the coldest eyes I had ever seen.

I felt an immediate revulsion. Everything about him was in sharp contrast to my pretty, delicate mother. His coarse-featured face was swarthy, his eyes the color of dull pewter, his mouth harsh, even as he tried to smile.

I stumbled to my feet, feeling threatened by his great height, his intimidating gaze. He was holding out his hand to me, and I was forced to put my own into it. I withdrew it hastily, wiping his clamminess on my pinafore. I thought at first my gesture undetected, but then I saw his mouth curl into a kind of sneer that frightened me.

Only Mr. Muir and I were conscious of this strange exchange that set once and for all our adversarial relationship, our mutual dislike. After that first meeting, I could not think of him without shuddering.

*C*hildren are much more sensitive to what goes on than the adults in their world realize. I soon sensed Nanny Grace did not like Henry Muir either. After Mama had flitted in and out of the nursery schoolroom for a quick visit before going off for an afternoon ride with Mr. Muir in his shiny black phaeton or out to an evening musicale or party, Nanny would shake her head grumbling, "Innocent as a lamb being led to the slaughter." I didn't know exactly what she meant, but I did feel uneasy about Mama's seeing so much of Mr. Muir.

When Mama, happy as a lark, declared they were going to marry, the Hazeltons put as good a face on it as they could. However, I don't think Uncle George and Aunt Evelyn were happy about the match either. Childless themselves, they treated my mother and I as if we had been their own, but they had to accept the marriage and that we would all be moving away to Muir's residence, Crossfield Grange, in a remote part of northern England.

The Hazeltons were unworldly, trusting people, and Henry Muir was a master of deceit. He had gone to great lengths to ingratiate himself with my mother's guardians until the betrothal was official.

I shall never forget the day of my mother's wedding. Sitting between Aunt Evelyn and Uncle George in the small, candlelit village church, watching my mother come down the aisle on the arm of a man I'd already begun to fear and distrust, I felt small and helpless. I wondered bleakly how she could look so radiant when my heart was near breaking.

But for all our private miseries, the four of us who loved Mama best saw her off on her wedding trip with Mr. Muir, not knowing how much all our lives would change.

While they were still abroad, Nanny and I traveled to Crossfield Grange. Ran and my Shetland pony, Betsy, were to be sent later.

With Nanny I always felt safe and secure, even during this tremendous upheaval. But at my first glimpse of the timbered Tudor house, with its overhanging roof and dormered windows, located on a rocky hillside and brooding over acres of rough, tuffetted moors, I felt a tremor of apprehension. The day itself was overcast; smoky gray clouds cast a depressing pall. Instinctively, I reached for Nanny's hand. I heard her quick intake of breath, as if she too found the sight daunting. Then she patted my hand. "It'll come right, dearie, by and by." However, her voice sounded quavery and unsure.

Inside, the house was also gloomy. Dark wood paneled and furnished with heavy, carved pieces, it was as depressing as the exterior. We found Crossfield Grange had a meager staff, only a cook, a downstairs maid, a scullery maid, and Mr. Muir's valet. Evidently, having been arranged beforehand, three of the servants from Briarwood Manor had been sent to work here—James, our footman; Marsden, the groom and coachman; and Lily, Mama's maid.

A week after our arrival, my mother and Mr. Muir returned, and I learned what direction my life would take. The day they came back I was called into the drawing room, where they were having tea. I had been outside romping with

Ran, and as he always followed me wherever I went, he came along into the room, his great paws and toenails making a scratching sound on the polished floors. It was then—at least to *me*—Mr. Muir showed his true colors.

At our entrance, he turned to Mama. "Surely, you don't allow that great brute of a dog in the house, Maria?"

Mama immediately looked anxious. She gave Muir a quick glance, then said to me in a gentle but worried voice, "Darling, why don't you take Ran out to the hall. Ask James to put him outside for now."

"But Ran is always allowed in at teatime," I said, puzzled by this unusual suggestion.

"Yes, darling, I know but—"

"Maria." Muir placed his hand over hers and said firmly, "Let me handle this, dear."

He turned his lusterless gaze on me. "Children should not argue with their elders, Challys." His voice was edged with ice. "Do as your mother told you."

I looked at Mama, expecting her to say something in Ran's behalf, but she only bit her lower lip and fiddled with the tea tray, nervously rearranging the sugar bowl and creamer.

Resentful that I should have to obey Muir, I tugged at Ran's collar and started pulling him toward the drawing room door. He resisted, and I had to drag him, sliding and whimpering, out to the hall. James, who had been standing in the hall, gave us both a sympathetic look and took the still-protesting dog.

As I turned to go back into the drawing room, I heard Muir remark to Mama, "Remember, my dear, children need a firm hand. A child must be trained to instant obedience. An unruly child is as unwelcome as an unruly animal."

I felt a hot rush of anger. Stepping back into the room, I glared at Muir and met a look that chilled me. There were triumph and satisfaction in his eyes, and also a threat.

That incident was an indication of what was to come. I soon found out Muir had no intention of including me in his new domestic arrangements. Within three weeks after their return, I was informed I would be going away, that Muir had enrolled me in a boarding school.

"A very fine institution for young ladies," he told my mother and me. "Its emphasis on discipline, orderliness, and deportment is just what Challys needs."

He turned a patronizing look on Mama. "Maybe you did not realize it, my dear, but it is certainly obvious to anyone else that your elderly relatives spoiled the child outrageously. She is self-willed and careless. All this is most deplorable, as I'm sure you'll agree. Challys will benefit greatly from this change."

"Of course, Henry," Mama murmured, but her eyes shining with unshed tears and her trembling mouth were not convincing. I knew sending me away was Muir's idea, not hers. I knew at that moment from then on *he,* not my tenderhearted mother, was to be in charge of all that concerned me.

A red-nosed, sniffling, tight-lipped Nanny Grace helped me pack my trunk. Loyal to my mother as she was, I knew Nanny did not want me to go. For both their sakes, I tried not to express the sense of abandonment I felt at being sent away. I attempted to tell myself staying at Crossfield Grange did not guarantee much happiness either. Still, as I drove away in the carriage on my way to Miss Elderberry's Academy, I pressed my face against the window, keeping in sight as long as possible the figures of Mama and Nanny Grace on the steps waving good-bye to me. We passed the bend in the road, and they were out of sight. I had just passed my thirteenth birthday; it was the end of my childhood.

It was hard to adjust to the strict regimen at boarding school after the easy, flexible way of life I had known at Briarwood Manor with the doting Lord and Lady Hazelton.

Still, I had to reconcile myself that, with my mother's remarriage, my life had changed irrevocably, and I had to make the best of the new circumstances. At school I soon made friends and settled in, reminding myself I could look forward to spending the school holiday with my dear mother in a few months.

To my dismayed disappointment that was not to be. At the end of the term, when I should have been leaving for the summer, the headmistress received a message from Mr. Muir that my mother was unwell and it would be best for me not to come to Crossfield Grange. I was desolate at the prospect of spending the holiday with a few other students whose parents were army or diplomatic personnel stationed in one of Great Britain's colonies too far away to visit. At the last minute, however, I was rescued. Evidently Nanny Grace had written the Hazeltons, and they came to get me.

I spent a happy enough holiday with them, for they did everything to make it so. After that one time, however, Muir sent word that I should remain at school during holidays if, for some reason, I couldn't come to Crossfields, explaining to the headmistress that "surely Challys would benefit from some added time given to her studies." In the thoughtless way of children, and with no one to prompt me, I failed to write to my elderly relatives, and gradually we lost touch.

As the school year continued, I began to worry about my mother more and more. I'd had only a few letters from her. In them she had said little about her new life at Crossfield Grange. Instead, her notes were filled with questions about my life at boarding school, and always ended with her hopes that I was happy and repeated reassurances of her love, even though it was necessary for us to be separated.

I didn't really understand why this had to be so. I decided I could manage to tolerate my stepfather if it were possible for me to stay with my mother and enjoy at least a semblance of our happy, old life together.

I was also puzzled why, if she was not seriously ill, I could not have gone to Crossfield Grange instead. In the past, when we had lived at Briarwood Manor, I had often sat on her bed, reading aloud to her when she had a headache or was slightly indisposed. Mama had always loved having me near her, no matter what.

When I was allowed to come to Crossfield Grange for the Christmas holidays, I got some idea of what I had not been able to read between the lines of her letters. I was certainly unprepared for the atmosphere I found upon my arrival there.

I had anticipated Mama would be at the stagecoach station to meet me. Instead, a newly hired, unsmiling coachman met me. When I asked about Marsden, he replied shortly, "Gone, Miss," then transferred my luggage to the rack on the end of the one-horse barouche. His brusque reply made me wonder what other changes I would find when I reached Crossfield Grange. Would James and Lily be gone as well?

When we arrived at the house and came to a stop in front, I drew a sigh of relief when I saw Nanny hurrying down the steps to greet me. I was out of the carriage in a flash, being hugged. While Nanny fussed, declaring I looked thin and needed fattening up, over her shoulder I saw a tall woman standing in the front door. Had Muir hired a housekeeper?

Nanny took my hand and we started up the steps together. At the top we halted, and I recognized something familiar about the woman's features, her severe expression. Her graying, dark hair was drawn plainly back from a center part. She wore a high-necked black dress with no adornment except for a large onyx brooch, glittering so like a big black beetle, I had to suppress a shudder.

"Good afternoon, Challys. I am your stepfather's sister. You may call me Aunt Sybil." Her voice was as cold as the hand she extended. As I touched it, I felt the same strange chill I had felt when I first met her brother.

I murmured something I hoped concealed my surprise and sounded polite.

Sybil Muir then turned to Nanny, and speaking as though used to giving her orders said, "You may take her up to see her mother for a few minutes, then Mr. Muir wants her down for tea at four."

As we went up the stairs, Nanny tried valiantly to prepare me. Mama had been ill, she whispered, so I was to speak quietly and was not to excite her or tire her out with too much chattering. That was indeed a difficult charge for one who was returning after a first separation from an adored mother.

In spite of Nanny's gentle warning, I was devastated by the startling changes in my beautiful, young mother.

I did not know my little brother's birth was imminent. Children were not told such things. I just thought how tiny and frail Mama looked in the big, canopied bed. For all her pallor she was still lovely, her glorious, golden-brown hair spread out like silk floss against the pillows.

She gave a little cry of welcome when she saw me and held out her arms to me. The ruffles of her shell-pink nightgown fell away from her arms as she did, and I was shocked to see how thin they were.

"Darling girl!" she called, but her voice seemed weak and lacked its usual lilt. I rushed over to her, snuggled in beside her on the downy quilt.

She kissed me and hugged me, told me how glad she was to see me, but even with my limited experience, I identified what I saw in her eyes as unhappiness.

A moment later, without knocking, Mr. Muir strode into the room. His harsh voice broke the spell of our happy reunion. "So you're here, Challys."

I felt my mother's thin fingers tighten convulsively on my arm.

He walked over, stood at the foot of the bed, and spoke to Mama without any softening of tone. "Well, Maria, you must not tire yourself with prolonged rejoicing over the prodigal's return." He used the term sarcastically.

To me he said, "Your mother needs rest. My sister says tea will be served in fifteen minutes, and you will join us in the drawing room." It was not anything like a cordial invitation. It was an order.

I would much rather have stayed and shared a quiet tea alone with my mother—I had so much I wanted to ask her and tell her—but Muir remained standing there as if waiting for me to obey. I glanced appealingly at Mama, hoping she would plead the same thing. Instead, an expression of anxiety came into her eyes, and she pressed my hand, gently urging, "Go along, darling. We shall have plenty of time to visit while you're here."

I could not help but notice she said *here,* not *home.* I think I knew then that Crossfield Grange did not feel like home to her either. I left reluctantly, tense and troubled. Something had entered my mother's room with Mr. Muir. It was fear.

A half hour later, I sat rigidly in the drawing room facing the Muirs, each ensconced in a straight-backed armchair flanking the black marble fireplace. I was very hungry after my long trip but couldn't eat my sandwiches or scones for having to answer the Muirs' rapid questions. I felt like a prisoner at the Inquisition.

"So what exactly are you studying, Challys?" Sybil asked, stirring her tea so that the silver spoon clinked against the side of the porcelain cup.

"Well, we have classes in grammar, botany, sums, music, and French—"

The spoon stopped abruptly.

"What? No religious or moral education?" she exclaimed, turning to her brother as if shocked. "That certainly was not the curriculum where *I* attended school."

"Oh, we do have chapel and Scripture study," I hastened to tell her.

She speared me with a withering glance. "It doesn't seem to have had much effect if you so quickly omit mentioning it."

She turned to her brother. "Surely, this is a lack you should investigate, Henry." She put down her teacup on the piecrust table beside her chair. "I think you should seriously consider sending Challys to my old school—Glenhaven in Scotland. There students are taught the fundamentals, not foolishness like French and dancing!"

Scotland! My stomach lurched at the thought of being sent even farther away from Mama. Desperately I tried to think of some way of improving the worth of my education at my present boarding school before Muir took it in his head to follow his sister's suggestion.

3

*E*ven the slight possibility that Muir would send me to a boarding school in Scotland might have motivated me to try to please my stepfather by good behavior in order that he would not consider such a drastic move, if it had not been for two separate but devastating discoveries.

After tea, I excused myself and went in search of my dear, devoted Ran. To my horror, I found him chained out near the stables, and I learned he was never allowed in the house. Seeing my approach, he went into a frenzy of joy, barking wildly, struggling to be free. I ran to him, threw my arms around his neck. Tears streamed down my face. "Poor old fellow. Poor boy," I said over and over as I caressed him and felt his warm tongue on my cheek.

When I finally got the chain loosened from his collar, he had a hard time standing. I realized his legs were weakened from lack of exercise and constant inactivity. The callous, young village youth who had replaced our old groom, Marsden, seemed indifferent when I complained about Ran's treatment. I was determined to protest to my stepfather. But there was more to come.

The second blow came when I found out that Muir had sold my pony. The next morning at breakfast, when I mentioned I thought I'd go for a ride, he offhandedly told me. I dropped my fork. "*Sold* Betsy?" I gasped.

"You're much too old for a pony, Challys. I shall look for a proper mount for you at the next horse fair."

Fury welled up within me in a fiery spasm. I pushed back my chair, stood up, fists clenched at my side. "You had no right to do that!"

"I had every right, young lady," he replied coldly. "All your mother's and your property now legally belongs to me."

I stared at my stepfather, hatred hardening my heart. Then I ran out of the dining room and rushed upstairs to my room where I flung myself on my bed, sobbing bitterly.

"I will never forgive him," I told Nanny Grace when she tried to comfort me.

All during those miserable three weeks I kept my distance from my stepfather, speaking only when spoken to, avoiding him as much as I could.

I took long walks on the desolate moors surrounding the house, trying to restore Ran's leg muscles as much as I could while I was there. He seemed to have lost his old energy and often limped far behind. Sometimes he just stopped and looked at me in a way that broke my heart. I would sit beside him, holding his head on my lap, weeping. Instinctively, I knew that the next time I came to Crossfield Grange Ran would be dead.

So went my first Christmas holiday in my new home.

Holiday? Certainly my time at Crossfield Grange that dark December was not worthy of the name.

My heart aches even now . . . remembering those dismal weeks. We were supposedly celebrating the most festive time of the year, but Crossfield Grange was a complete contrast to the joyous Christmases we enjoyed at Briarwood Manor. There, the rooms were gaily decorated with fragrant cedar boughs and holly, bright with red berries. The delicious smells of baking pies, roasting goose, and all the other tantalizing, delightful aromas associated with the holiday filled the whole house. Sweet-scented candles glowed in every window, welcoming the constant flow of visitors arriving for parties and balls. Music, the sound of dancing feet, and the excited cheers when the Yule log was brought in or the Christmas pudding, aflame and smelling heavenly of spices and rum, was placed on the table echoed through the house.

On Christmas Eve, snow was usually falling. Just at dark, carolers from the village were heard outside singing "O Little Town of Bethlehem" or "God Rest Ye Merry, Gentlemen," and we stood on the terrace, shivering, listening. Then Aunt Evelyn had cups of steaming cider brought out for the carolers. A little later we went to church, where the glorious story of the Christ child's birth and the shepherds' arrival at the stable was read. After riding home through the frosty night, we opened presents around the tree with its sparkling candles.

At Crossfields there was no such gaiety, no sense of the holiday spirit or the meaning of the holiday.

I returned to school after the holiday feeling depressed. Perhaps in the spring things would be better.

They were not. In fact, I found things were much worse.

To my dismay, I learned that not only had Sybil Muir extended her visit, she was now established as a permanent member of the household. I no longer had easy access to Mama. We were never alone. We were always in the company of either Mr. Muir or his dour sister. My mother seemed smaller, more fragile, intimidated not only by her husband but also by his sister. She kept to her room, often to her bed, and rarely joined us for tea or dinner. The piano remained closed, and the mother I had known, who laughed, danced, and sang, seemed to have disappeared. A kind of invisible yet palpable check seemed to discourage all spontaneity.

Again I returned to school heavyhearted.

The one bright spot in all this was the news of the arrival

of a baby brother. This announcement was delivered to me by the headmistress. The excitement it brought was diluted with the further information that his birth had taken all my mother's strength and that I was not to come home until the end of the term. Unhappy as that made me, I was assured I could come for his christening that summer.

Disappointments such as this were becoming routine in my new life. It was not until much later that I realized Muir had contrived deliberately to set me apart from my mother and little brother. If he thought he could alienate me from my mother and brother, however, he was sadly mistaken. When I was at Crossfield Grange, I tried in every way to make up for the long periods I was not there.

The baby was duly christened Tyrone. I had the privilege of holding him during the ceremony at the village church because my mother was still not well. Assisted by a young maid, Nanny Grace had taken over his care, and while I was there, I was constantly in the nursery. Ty, as Nanny and I began to call him, was a beautiful baby, favoring my mother, thank goodness, with tufts of red-gold curls, big, dark eyes, rosy cheeks, and a sweet smile. I adored him from the minute I saw him, and I was very sad to leave him when my summer holiday ended and I had to go back to school.

How strong the bond between us grew would be proven later. During the next two years, even though I was away from him for months at a time, my little brother grew dear and precious to me.

Because of my own affection for Ty and how remarkable I thought him, I found it very odd Mr. Muir paid little attention to his son and heir. He seemed indifferent as Ty grew into a sturdy little boy with obvious intelligence and a lovable personality. All the things Nanny and I thought marvelous about Ty seemed of no interest to Mr. Muir. I questioned Nanny about this.

"Most men don't think much of babies," she said. "When

he's older and running about, talking and such, Mr. Muir'll likely pay him more mind."

However, from the lift of her eyebrow and the curl of her lip when she said this, I didn't think Nanny really believed that would happen. Although she never said it in so many words, I could tell by a sniff or a shrug that Nanny did not care much for either of the Muirs. She was absolutely loyal and devoted, however, to my mother and Ty. Sad as I was to part with Mama and Ty each time a holiday was up and I had to return to school, I felt better knowing Nanny was there looking after both of them.

Still, the situation at Crossfields remained nearly always on my mind. I worried about Ty growing up in that stern and loveless environment with such a father.

Also, now that I was getting older and had my own romantic fantasies, I often wondered how my mother, with her delightful sense of humor and love for music, dancing, and company, had ever seen anything to love about Mr. Muir. He seemed the most humorless, negative man I'd ever known. Of course, he and I had little to say to each other ever. I had never forgiven him for selling my pony or the cruel way Ran had been exiled. It still hurt me to think about it. The dear old dog had been put down because of his deteriorating condition. I still missed him.

When I was at Crossfield Grange, we lived in a suspended state of truce. I knew Mr. Muir had the power to make my life even more impossible, so I kept my tongue and avoided him as much as I could when I was there. This was not difficult. Muir was often away. Nanny told me he was sometimes gone for days at a time, with no explanation to my mother or the staff. He came and went at will, leaving his formidable sister in charge. When Muir was absent, Mama usually did not come down, and I had to endure long dinner hours with "Aunt Sybil." She asked me questions about my studies and was critical and disparaging about everything and everybody.

Crossfield Grange was not a happy place. Indeed, if it hadn't been for Mama, Ty, and Nanny Grace, school would have been preferable to my time spent there.

It was Nanny who kept me informed of every detail of Ty's progress—his first tooth, his first word, his first steps. I read every word, longing to be there myself, even though that would have meant enduring the Muirs.

Over the next few years, it was Nanny who alerted me to the dire events that began taking place at Crossfields. Gradually her hints became stronger. Eventually she reported Muir's indifference to my mother and brother had become worse: unkindness, neglect.

As a young widow, my mother had been left a sizable fortune by my father, who had been an only child as well as the favorite nephew of an earl. Mama had brought that wealth to her second marriage. But I learned from Nanny that Muir was going through it with such rapidity that soon nothing would be left. Certainly there would be no inheritance for Ty if things continued unchecked.

During my final year at school, I learned how bad our financial situation had become when the headmistress called me into her parlor. With considerable tact she informed me that my tuition had not been paid for months. Regretfully, she said, if my fees were not caught up at once, I would not be able to return to school for the next term. Humiliated and shocked, I stammered that there must be some mistake. I promised I would write my mother immediately about the matter.

I explained the situation in a hastily written letter to my mother and sent it off by the next post.

A week went by, ten days, and still there was no answer from Mama.

I was again called into the headmistress's office.

"I am very sorry, Miss Pomoroy. I can't imagine why I haven't heard anything from my mother," I began in a shaky voice.

"Our contact has been with your stepfather, Mr. Muir. Perhaps you best write directly to him, Challys. He gave me the impression your mother was an invalid. Maybe it would be better not to disturb her, whatever the problem is."

The idea that Muir had described my mother as a helpless invalid infuriated me. Although she was much changed, *intimidated* would be a better description of her situation. She was still fully capable of understanding my tuition had not been paid and of remedying it. If she knew, she would be distressed that I had suffered such embarrassment.

I murmured something, and Miss Pomoroy kindly excused me.

In that same day's mail I received a letter from Nanny. In it she said that things were entirely out of hand at Crossfield Grange. She asked if I could possibly come home.

Dearest child,

I hope you can find a way to come to Crossfields as soon as possible. I cannot describe vividly enough the extent of what has been happening here. Half the staff has left because their wages have not been paid. Cook, who is too old to go elsewhere, remains, as does Muir's surly valet, for reasons of his own. Of the few who came with us from Briarwood Manor, only Lily and I remain. I stay because of my devotion to your dear mama. Lily, though young enough to easily get another lady's maid position, has become engaged to a local farmer. She'll probably go when they marry. Of course, I shall never leave as long as I'm needed, but something must be done. I don't know what else to tell you, except please come as soon as you can. See for yourself.

Ever,
Your loving Nanny Grace

Frightened, because I knew Nanny would not exaggerate, I determined I must leave at once for Crossfield Grange and find out exactly what was going on there. Pleading an emergency at home, I went to the headmistress for permission. Since she already knew something was amiss in my family, she granted my request. I had the further embarrassment of having to ask her to lend me traveling money, assuring her it would be paid back along with overdue tuition fees.

When I arrived at Crossfield Grange, I found the situation far worse than I could have imagined or than Nanny had described.

*I*n the months since I had been home on summer holiday, Sybil Muir had departed, driven away by Muir's drinking bouts and rages. My mother, in a state of nerves, remained secluded in her room most of the time. Muir, it seemed, spent long periods of time away in London at gaming houses, drinking and gambling away what was left of my mother's fortune. He was not at Crossfield Grange when I arrived, and I had time to assess the dire state of affairs.

Everything was in disarray. The estate was beginning to deteriorate. The staff, demoralized and without direction, had become lazy. The whole house had an air of neglect.

To make matters worse, at age four Ty had begun having frequent and severe bouts of asthma, which Nanny felt were brought on by the stress created by my stepfather's behavior. In spite of all Nanny Grace's efforts to protect him from the bleak situation at Crossfield Grange, my little brother, like my mother, had become Muir's victim.

The evening I arrived Ty was suffering from an attack, aggravated by his excitement at seeing me. I sat with Nanny in his bedroom until he went to sleep. Nanny kept a kettle of steaming water on the spirit burner near his bedside to help him breathe easier.

I was appalled by all I had discovered. "Whatever shall we do?" I asked Nanny.

Nanny shook her head sorrowfully. There seemed no solution for all the problems. My mother, she said, had given up. Nanny, herself, now getting old and rheumatic, had all she could do caring for Ty.

Late that night, we heard my stepfather return. I went to the stair landing, ready to march down and face him, explain to him the reasons for my arrival, and demand from him some explanation for the way he was treating my mother and Ty. But when he roared for his manservant and called my mother downstairs, demanding a bottle and dinner at once, Nanny held me back. "No use, dearie," she whispered. "It will only make things worse." Now, I saw firsthand what my dear mother and my precious little brother had been enduring. Then and there I promised myself, whatever it took, I would free them from this unbearable situation.

Nanny and I sat up most of that night discussing possible ways out of this seemingly hopeless dilemma. Toward dawn, we decided on a plan. When she felt it was warranted, she would send me a message that the time was right to put it into action. It was a reckless and dangerous plan for a girl of eighteen and an old woman to devise and initiate. However we both realized that the desperate plight of my mother and brother, helpless to act on their own behalf, demanded extreme measures.

Nanny did not need to point out to me the obvious. My mother was failing, fading before our eyes. She was thin to emaciation, her once beautiful eyes sunken in her hollow-cheeked face. Neither of us could bear to admit aloud that she had lost the will to live, probably even hoped to die. She blamed herself for the misery she had brought on us all by her marriage to Muir.

If I had allowed myself to speak of or to dwell on these realities, I would have lost heart completely. I could not give way. Everything now depended on me.

The day before I was to return to school, Nanny motioned me into Mama's room. Mama sat up in bed and beckoned me closer. Weak as she was, I found her very agitated. She drew a small packet of money from under her pillow and pressed it into my hand. In a hoarse voice she told me she had secretly sent Nanny to sell some of the inherited pieces of jewelry she had kept hidden from Muir, afraid he would confiscate them and use them to pay off his gambling debts. Since English law decreed a married woman's property, money, and possessions belonged to her husband, Muir already had access to and control over the money Mama received in monthly cheques from my father's estate. Selling her jewelry was the only way Mama could get any money without going through Muir.

Mama also furtively slipped me a chamois bag containing her set of diamond and sapphire pendant and earrings, a gift from my father on their wedding day.

"These would rightfully come to you anyway, my darling. I'm afraid if left here they might disappear upon my death, so best you take them now." She whispered even though Muir was noisily sleeping off his latest drunken stupor downstairs.

"I don't know what will happen in the future, my darling, and this is all I can do at present," Mama said, her large eyes haunted and brimming with tears. "God willing, I will find a way so that you and Ty will not be destitute but—"

She paused, biting her lower lip to keep from breaking down. "Forgive me for bringing this disaster upon you. If only I'd known—"

She began to cry and I took her in my arms, rocking her gently, trying to soothe her. Her body felt as delicate and weightless as a little bird's.

It hurt me to see my mother so beset, her eyes ringed with purple shadows, her once beautiful face haggard, her expression tense and troubled. Rage and vengeance toward the man who had caused this terrible change in her rose within me.

"If anything happens to me, Lyssa, you must take care of Ty."

"Oh, Mama, don't say that. You're not going to die!" I cried out, but my words held no conviction.

Her hands clutched mine convulsively and I almost winced with pain. "Listen to me!" she pleaded earnestly, her eyes burning. "Nanny's too old. It's up to *you*. You must see he is safe. Promise me, no matter what, you will be responsible for Ty. Promise?"

Tears rushed and spilled down my cheeks and I nodded. "I promise."

She sighed, then seemed to lose what strength she had mustered to command that promise. Her hold on me loosened, and she fell back against her bed pillows obviously exhausted. Weakly, she instructed me to pay my school fees and repay the money Miss Pomoroy had lent me for traveling expenses, to keep the rest of the money, and not to hesitate to sell the jewels if ever I found myself in circumstances of need.

Nanny came in just then to say the carriage was waiting to take me to the stagecoach station. Heartsick with grief, Mama and I bade farewell to each other, not knowing if it might be the last time. I hugged and kissed Ty and said goodbye to Nanny, with a silent confirmation of commitment to our plan. Then, with deep foreboding, I left to return to school.

I was back at school hardly a fortnight when word came of my mother's death.

The sad day of my mother's funeral is etched forever in my mind. It was a desolate, overcast day, heavy with clouds. Rain-blown wind whipped at my cape, tugged at my bonnet strings, tore the remaining leaves from the trees that lined the cemetery road and sent them scattering across granite headstones.

Holding Ty's little hand, I clung to Nanny's with my other and looked across the gaping gravesite, into which they had just lowered Mama's coffin, at the harsh face of my stepfather. How I despised him, the source of Mama's misery. Surely he had also hastened her death. I vowed I would do anything and everything in my power to rescue my little brother from the control and power of this evil man.

Since we assumed Muir had notified Lord and Lady Hazelton of Mama's death, they being her closest relatives, we were puzzled that they had not come for the funeral. Not a letter, a telegram, or even a wreath of flowers for her grave had been sent. I tried to explain their absence away, telling myself the shock of the news, their grief, or the distance of the trip had prevented them from coming for the funeral. Perhaps their age or physical condition had also been a factor.

With the long day finally over and Ty tucked in bed, Nanny and I stayed up until midnight making our final plans. It was decided I would write to the Hazeltons and ask their permission to come with Ty to stay with them. Because of my memories of a happy childhood at Briarwood Manor, I felt sure they would welcome us. My confidence in their caring love for us went so far as to predict they might even adopt Ty and make him their heir.

Until I heard from them, I would return to school to finish my last year, preparing me for a teaching or governess position, which I would certainly need. Although my penniless plight was in some ways the same as Ty's, it was also different. Muir had gone through any inheritance I might have received from my own father through Mama. Without Mama's fortune, I was left without a dowry and so with no prospects for a prestigious marriage, an unenviable position for a young woman, though marriage was far from my mind.

Muir had already informed me that he would not be paying any more of my tuition, that it was—in his words—"high time you started earning your keep for all the years I've supported you."

I had to check my anger at this and not fling back at him the truth, that it was my mother's money that had paid for everything. There was too much at stake. Outwardly meek, I accepted his dictum, glad that Mama had given me money for tuition.

Back at school, as soon as Nanny sent word "when," I would leave school, meet her with Ty at Tynley Junction, and take Ty on to Briarwood Manor.

Nanny's urgent message came sooner than I expected and before I had received a response from Briarwood Manor. We would have to move very quickly, she wrote, before Muir came out of the most recent of the stupors into which he had been drinking himself since Mama's funeral. Nanny had requested and been given permission to take Ty with her to visit her widowed sister at her cottage in Kent for a few days to comfort the little boy on the loss of his mother. What Muir would do when he sobered up and found all three of us had disappeared I dared not imagine.

I would cross that bridge when I came to it. The important thing for me to concentrate on was meeting Nanny and taking Ty. Once Ty and I got to Briarwood Manor, I felt sure Uncle George would do whatever was legally necessary to safeguard us, even though he might be shocked by both our arrival and our circumstances.

And such now was the mission of my journey. I was on my way to carry out my part of the plan Nanny and I had agreed on before my mother's death.

Suddenly Lady Bethune's sharp voice jerked me back to the present. "So, young lady, I suppose you are on your way from London after a whirl of a social season."

Still preoccupied, I looked at her blankly, her comment seemed totally unconnected to my troubling thoughts.

As I hesitated, she frowned, her mouth pursed petulantly. "I find it strange that a young lady of quality like yourself is traveling without a chaperone, or at least a maid."

She paused, as if awaiting an explanation, and I realized

that while I had been preoccupied with thoughts of my uncertain future, Lady Bethune must have been surveying me carefully, drawing her own conclusions about my age, status, and probable reason for traveling out of London on this miserable morning. She would have been surprised, I was sure, to know she had drawn all the wrong conclusions, even though my general appearance, the fine material of my well-made traveling outfit, and my upper-class accent indicated much of what she conjectured about me was true. In her wildest imaginings, she surely would not have conceived that I was actually a *fugitive,* that I had lied to the headmistress of my school, that I was on my way to meet my accomplice and complete my part of a criminal conspiracy to kidnap a little boy.

Demurely as I could, I replied, "No, Lady Bethune, I have not been enjoying a social season in London. I am recently bereaved and am on my way to meet my brother and travel with him to our relatives' home where we shall live now."

She seemed somewhat taken aback by this reply, and as I turned again to stare out the window, she was, momentarily at least, abashed enough by her mistaken assumptions not to initiate further conversation.

The closer we got to the village where Nanny's sister lived, where I was to meet Nanny and Ty, the more nervous I became. Suppose something had happened to prevent their coming? Perhaps Ty had suffered one of his asthma attacks. What if, heaven forbid, Muir had uncovered our plan somehow and snatched Ty back for whatever devious reasons of his own? Involuntarily, I shivered and, too late, saw that Lady Bethune was still watching me curiously.

As the coach suddenly lurched to a shuddering stop, I realized we were at Tynley Junction. My heart was pounding as I gathered my skirts and pressed forward, impatient for the coach door to open. It was jerked wide, letting in a cold, damp wind, and the driver shouted, "All out that's stoppin' 'ere! We got twenty minutes' rest whilst we change horses."

Lady Bethune, peering out the window next to her, exclaimed, "What a hovel the station looks. What a dismal place for a rest stop. Good thing we brought our own tea, Thompson."

Then she glanced sharply at me. "And where do you think you're going, young lady?"

I thought it none of her business, but having been taught to be polite to my elders, I replied mildly, "This is where I'm to meet my brother."

"Ah! And how old is your brother?"

"Five, almost six."

She looked aghast. "An infant! You mean we're to have a babe on our hands for the rest of the journey? I hope he's well behaved. I can't abide noisy, spoiled children."

I was immediately on the defensive, and I replied coldly, "My brother is *very* well behaved, I assure you. And bright and sweet natured as well," which was more than I could have said for *her.*

Though her remark had made me dread the rest of the long journey ahead, I was determined not to let a fussy old woman, used to having her own way as well as her own private carriage, bother me. I had come this far, overcoming hurdles she could never dream of, and had only the second part of our plan to complete—the journey to the blessed safety of Briarwood Manor.

My heart melted at the sight of Nanny, huddled in a voluminous hooded cape, sitting on a wooden bench under the shelter of the dripping overhang of the dilapidated stagecoach station. Ty was cuddled close, Nanny's arm protectively around him. When he saw me, he jumped up and ran to me, grabbing my waist as I leaned down to hug him.

"Lyssa! Lyssa, you've come!" he said over and over, lifting his round, rosy-cheeked face to look up at me, smiling.

Nanny hobbled toward us, and my heart ached to see how bent she was. She seemed to have aged even in the few weeks since my mother's death.

"Dearest child, thank God you've come. I've been worried. Afraid something would happen—"

"I know, Nanny, I know. I have too, but everything has worked out as we planned. It will be all right now. As soon as we get to Briarwood Manor, we'll be fine."

I wished I felt as certain of the outcome of this risky venture as I claimed. There was still the matter of not having received a response from Briarwood Manor, and in the back of my mind I was troubled by the knowledge that the plan was built on lies, no matter how necessary they were, no matter how critical the cause.

"And you, Nanny, will you be all right? You're not going back to Crossfield Grange, are you?"

She shook her head vigorously. "Never! Not to that blackguard or to that place that was your dear mother's prison."

"All aboard that's goin' wi' us to Dorset!" The harsh call of the stagecoach driver rang out through the misty air.

"You best go now, my dearies," Nanny said, her voice cracking a little. "I won't worry about you two anymore. In a short while you'll reach the home of your dear mother's relatives, where I know you'll be safe."

We hugged.

"Be a good lad, won't you, Ty? Don't give your sister any trouble. Just do as you're told, won't you?"

"Yes, Nanny!" Ty nodded, looking from one to the other of us, his little brow puckered with concern, for we were both crying.

"Here, I've fixed a wee basket of goodies in case the stage is late and you get hungry." Nanny thrust a small wicker hamper into my hands. "I know when you reach the manor they'll have a feast for you."

I didn't want to tell Nanny I had not yet heard from Lady Hazelton. When I had received Nanny's urgent message that we had to put our plan into action immediately, I just came. There was no use worrying her.

After hugs all around, we took leave of Nanny, her "God

bless" following us. Holding Ty tightly by the hand, I walked back toward the waiting stagecoach. Lifting Ty up over the high step into the carriage, I saw we had gathered four new passengers for the rest of the trip. I noticed Lady Bethune's martyred look as she moved to the end of her side of the seat. She gave several exasperated sighs as the portly Thompson was squeezed between her and a stout man who, with much huffing and puffing, wedged himself into the leftover space.

A couple with pinched faces and disapproving glances made room for me and Ty as we boarded. Contrary to my belief that children were universally loved, I discovered that others felt as Muir did. The fourth new passenger had opted to ride on top next to the driver and his helper.

I felt Lady Bethune's curiosity double as we settled ourselves. I helped Ty off with his bulky jacket and removed the knitted cap I recognized as Nanny's handiwork. I looked down fondly at my handsome little brother, ruffled his russet-gold curls affectionately. He looked up at me with eyes so much like our mother's I felt my throat tighten. He smiled, showing his dimples, and I pulled him onto my lap with a hug, returning Lady Bethune's stare, as if to say, who could resist this dear little fellow?

Totally unaware he might be the target of unwelcoming thoughts, Ty grinned happily at the other occupants of the carriage as he munched contentedly on the apple I dug out for him from Nanny's basket. It was growing dark as we got underway, and the coach moved at a fast clip in spite of the fog and drizzle.

Having earlier been roused out of his warm bed into the chilly morning, Ty's head soon began to nod, and leaning against my shoulder, he went to sleep. Troubled with worried thoughts, I was not as lucky. At least we were on our way to safety. Eventually I began to relax, and lulled by the rocking motion of the carriage coupled with my own exhaustion and stress, I drifted off.

Suddenly, I was startled awake by a crashing jolt. The terrified screams of my fellow passengers rent the air as the carriage swayed, shuddered, then tilted precariously. Everyone slid to one side. I gripped Ty, who had awakened and now began to cry.

"We've had an accident!" someone shouted.

The man on the other side of the coach struggled free from a tangle of skirts, hatboxes, and reticules, and managed to scramble up. He pushed open the door and peered out into the murky morning.

"I'll see what's happened," he announced to no one in particular, then disappeared from sight. To our horror, there followed an ear-splitting cry and a splash. Sickeningly I realized the stagecoach must be overturned and pitched sideways, suspended over water.

We heard the frightened horses shrieking in terror. As they lurched to right themselves, they sent tremors through the dangerously tipped carriage. Inside there were only the sounds of muffled groans, rapid breathing. We were all too afraid to speak.

5

*F*inally the other male passenger's steady voice broke through our collective fright.

"We must be very still or the whole carriage will turn over. Be calm, or none of us will make it. Someone is bound to come and help us."

I felt Ty's clinging arms tighten almost to a stranglehold around my neck. I patted his quivering little body and murmured soothingly, hoping to keep him quiet. My own common sense echoed the other passenger's cautionary warning that the slightest motion might send the whole coach and its occupants hurtling into the icy water I knew was below. I closed my eyes, prayed silently, and tried to comfort Ty.

I don't know how long we hung there, literally between life and death. Maybe it was only minutes; it felt like hours. The waiting seemed endless. However long it took, eventually the man who had spoken those reassuring words was right. The coach driver's husky voice called to us, "Hold on, now, we're comin' to get you out!" A few seconds later his head, illuminated by the lantern he was carrying, emerged into the carriage.

"Folks, we've got the horses unhitched and moved away. We've put rocks under the wheels so as not to tip this whole thing over. Now, we'll get you out of here one at a time. Move slowly, carefully. Easy does it."

I was in agony as I kept Ty still, holding my breath, afraid nearly to breathe. First, the whimpering Thompson was guided forward, Lady Bethune shoving her from behind. Then "milady" herself, with no hesitation at all, followed. Next, the prune-faced woman on my right, her eyes wide with fear, was helped by her stoic husband through the carriage door. Then it was my turn. With Ty in my arms, I inched on the slanted floor of the coach toward the open door.

"Hand me the lad," the driver ordered.

I did so, releasing Ty from my stiffened fingers.

"There you go, laddie!" the driver said as he took Ty from me. A minute later the driver was back. "Hurry, now, miss, don't know how long we can keep this vehicle from slidin'."

I felt strong hands grip my upper arms, pull me up roughly, and swing me around. Then at last I felt my boot soles on the soggy ground of the riverbank and knew I was safely out of the wrecked carriage. I looked around and saw Ty standing with the other rescued passengers a little farther up, near the road. Slipping a bit on the rain-soaked grass and mud, I made my way up to join them.

We were all a little dizzy from relief. On the edge of hysteria, I suppose. Some were making humorous remarks about our mishap, others laughing, if uneasily. We all knew we had barely escaped death.

But in a few minutes it began to drizzle, dampening the strained humor of the situation. The attempts at jokes turned to grumbles and complaints, in some cases to mumbled swearing with little care that ladies and children were within earshot.

My skirt hem was already wet, and I was shivering. Ty was

wide awake now and finding it all a great adventure. We women stood a little apart, and the male passengers joined the driver and his helper, huddling in a small circle discussing the problem.

An earlier storm had blown down tree limbs. The driver surmised a large fallen tree branch might have been the obstacle the stagecoach's wheels struck, overturning us. Either that or a dislodged boulder that, loosened by the soaked ground, had rolled into the road.

We were stranded, it seemed, in the middle of nowhere. I looked around at the unfamiliar countryside. Below the embankment where we were all gathered like bedraggled refugees, the river, swollen with rain, rushed in a mighty current, the huge hulk of the half-sunken stagecoach barely visible. It looked like a beached whale. In the distance I saw the outline of an arched bridge we had been about to cross when the accident happened.

After what seemed like a great deal of time, the driver came over and informed us that he was sending his helper to hike to an inn, which was a regular stagecoach stop. There he could get us help. The driver was sure they'd send a wagon to fetch us and give us shelter for the night. It would be morning before they could get the damaged coach righted.

"Then, we'll get word to the next stagecoach station, and they'll dispatch another coach and have you ladies and gents on your way 'fore long," he said heartily.

I'm not sure any of us believed him, but there was nothing we could do but agree that his was as good an idea as any. We watched the man set off with one of the only two lanterns. As his lonely figure merged into the darkness and disappeared, I believe a common mood of depression about our plight settled on the group. Standing there in the misty chill, none of us thought things could be worse, but we were all wrong. Soon the drizzle turned into rain, and within minutes it began to rain steadily. In time the rain became a downpour. There was absolutely nothing we could do but stand there and become soaked. I wrapped my pelisse as best I could around Ty, who had begun to shiver violently. What this exposure might do to him, given his susceptibility to taking cold, added to my other worries.

We were all miserable by the time we saw lanterns bobbing in the distance. As the lights moved closer, we could see our driver's helper arriving with a man driving a large farm wagon pulled by two workhorses.

Drenched by the rain and shuddering from the chill, we were herded into the wagon and seated on the rough boards that lined each side. My bonnet was hanging around my neck from its strings, and without its covering, my hair was dripping wet. As we bumped along the rutted road, I hunched over Ty, hoping my body heat would offer him some protection from the cold. By the time we reached the inn, however, Ty's breathing was labored, and with a sinking heart I knew that he had caught a bad chill.

We entered the main room of the inn where a fire had been started for our benefit. The innkeeper's wife, a stout, florid-faced woman, introduced herself as Mrs. Brindle. She made noisy, clucking sounds of sympathy as she ladled out bowls of warm broth. I tried to get Ty to take a few mouthfuls but from his eyes, glassy with fever, and his skin, hot to the touch, I knew I had a new problem. To ward off a serious illness, I knew I had to get him in bed at once. I asked the innkeeper's wife if there was a room available.

She took one look at Ty and said, "Come along."

I followed her up the stairway with Ty in my arms.

She showed me into a small but neat room and turned back the patchwork quilt on the bed. The linen was fresh, the coverlet clean.

As I lay Ty down, his small body was shaking. Mrs. Brindle gave him a sharp look and said to me, "The lad's caught a bad chill, for sure. You best keep him snug and warm. I'll have Peg heat a brick, wrap it in flannel, and slip it under the sheets. That'll warm him up quick."

She bustled out of the room and I heard her heavy, clumping footsteps going back downstairs. I was filled with apprehension. From Nanny's descriptions of Ty's other illnesses, I recognized he was very sick.

A few minutes later a sleepy-eyed young woman appeared, obviously resentful that she had been awakened to help with a crowd of unexpected travelers. She carried a flannel-wrapped square, which she held out to me. With poor grace and a sullen look she said, "Here 'tis."

I took it from her, murmuring my thanks, too worried about my brother to say more.

There was an extra quilt in the blanket box at the foot of the bed, so I took off my own wet, outer clothes and wrapped myself in it. I drew the one straight chair up to the side of the bed where Ty lay, flushed and breathing laboriously.

Keeping a lonely vigil through the night, I wondered what in the world I would do if Ty were too sick to continue our journey. Toward dawn I got up, stretched my stiff muscles, and walked over to the window.

The morning sky was lighting, but it still looked ominous. The old adage "Red sky at morning, sailors take warning" spun through my head. More storms ahead. I glanced anxiously over to the bed where Ty restlessly slept. Leaning over him, I placed my hand on his forehead. It was burning hot.

I knew, whether or not the stagecoach company sent another carriage for the stranded passengers, my little brother was too sick to continue our journey. We would have to stay here until he was well.

Of course, staying at the inn meant using more of the small sum of money I was hoarding so carefully. Extra days of lodging and meals would speedily reduce the amount that had remained after I had paid my overdue tuition, and if I had to summon a doctor for Ty, he would have to be paid as well. Still, it had to be done for Ty's sake. He certainly couldn't travel in his condition.

How would I get word to the Hazeltons? After receiving

my letter telling them what I intended to do, Aunt Evelyn would be beside herself with worry if we did not show up as planned. I must send a message explaining the delay. Perhaps, knowing Ty was ill, Uncle George would send his own carriage and coachman for us.

I would have to ask the stagecoach driver to take my letter, paying him of course, taking the chance he *would* post it, not just pocket the money.

Even knowing that Uncle George would generously reimburse me for expenses incurred, I still felt a gnawing anxiety about our predicament. That was nothing, however, compared to the horror I experienced a moment later—my purse was missing! A frantic search through my skirt, jacket, and pelisse was futile.

In all the confusion after the accident, my mind had been preoccupied with getting out of the carriage safely and making sure Ty was okay. I must have dropped my purse somehow. I couldn't think, couldn't remember, if it had been on my lap, beside me on the seat—where. It didn't matter. All the money I had left was gone! How could I have been so careless? What was I to do?

Then I remembered Mama's jewels. My stomach lurched. I felt sick, dizzy. I reached for the small chamois bag that I had tied around my waist under my petticoats. In it was all that was left of her jewelry, my insurance against disaster to be used only in an emergency.

It would be easy to say this was it, but I knew better. Priceless heirloom jewels could not be used for common tender. You didn't pay a country inn bill with valuable diamonds and sapphires. An innkeeper would not even know the value of such gems. No, the jewels would not solve my present problem, nor was I ready to part with them—at least not yet. Once the Hazeltons knew of our situation, I had no doubt they would take care of all our expenses. My main concern had to be Ty, getting him well.

I went back over to the bed and looked down at my little

brother. My heart swelled for him. The full weight of the tremendous responsibility that was mine pressed down on me, as did my feelings of inadequacy at the thought of having to protect and care for him. I sank to my knees beside the bed and prayed earnestly for guidance. My task to get us safely to Briarwood Manor seemed impossible, but "with God, all things are possible." I had to rely on that bedrock of faith, as well as keep my head and use my wits.

A tap on the door drew my attention. I opened it to a kerchiefed maid, a different maid than the one who had brought up the heated brick the night before. This one was a country lass, rosy cheeked and cheerful.

"Mornin', miss." She bobbed a curtsey. "The mistress says to tell you she's servin' breakfast now for the passengers. Another stagecoach's come over from the junction to carry the passengers who was dumped last night. They'll be on their way in an hour, she says."

"I must have a word with your mistress," I said as calmly as I could. "Would you mind staying here with my little brother for a few minutes while I speak to her?"

"For sure, miss." The girl nodded, walked over to the bed and peeked down at Ty. His cheeks were red from fever, his russet curls a tangled mass against the linen.

"He's a bonnie one, ain't he?" she whispered, meeting my gaze. "I'm gettin' married meself come next month, and I want to have a half dozen of me own."

Sensing her love for children, I felt I was leaving Ty in good hands and went quietly out of the room. As I went downstairs, I rehearsed what I would say to Mrs. Brindle. She had certainly seemed kind and helpful the night before. That, however, was when she'd believed I was a paying guest. It might be a different kettle of fish when she knew I had no money. I was sure she had assumed from my dress and speech that I had the means to pay for our room and Ty's care for the length of time necessary for his recovery. Innkeepers were in business for profit, not charity.

The innkeeper himself, Mr. Brindle, whom I had hardly noticed nor spoken to the night before, was much in evidence this morning. He had the look of a drinker. I'd learned the signs from seeing Muir drunk. Mr. Brindle's face was blotched, his nose bulbous, his eyes bloodshot and bleary. Obviously it was his wife who ran things. Mr. Brindle was talking in a loud voice with the stagecoach driver, waving in one hand a tankard that I guessed contained ale not coffee.

Lady Bethune and the other passengers were seated in the taproom at one long trestle table. I cast a wary eye at Thompson, who looked vaguely uncomfortable. This was probably the first time she had sat at the same table with her employer.

I found myself wondering if any of the others had found themselves in a predicament similar to my own. Surely not all of them had been thinking about gathering their belongings, though perhaps each had held on to whatever seemed most important at the time. To most it *would* have been their money, not having a small child to look after. I had been most concerned about Ty.

The smell of sausage frying rose tantalizingly to my nose, and I realized I was hungry. Great platters of potatoes, fluffy eggs, rolls, thick slices of homemade bread, and mounds of creamy butter were being passed around, and everyone was helping themselves and eating heartily.

I put the thought of food out of my mind. I had more urgent matters to deal with.

6

I glanced around the room for the innkeeper's wife. I saw her through the doorway into the kitchen. She was red faced, bustling about, bossing the cook, and overseeing the serving.

Then for some reason my gaze met Lady Bethune's. She was studying me speculatively. The thought crossed my mind to confide in her. Most certainly *she* would have held on to her purse. All I needed to do was mention Lord and Lady Hazeltons' names to assure her that she would be repaid. But as my gaze lingered on her elegantly held head, the faint disdain I saw in her expression and her air of detachment from the rest of the now convivial group of survivors caused me to recoil.

I couldn't. I was too proud.

Besides, Lady Bethune—well, she had not impressed me as the most compassionate person in the world. She was likely too self-centered to care for the problems of others, not one who would readily offer either sympathy or monetary help. I would not ask for either. I would face this myself in the most dignified, honorable way I could.

I made another decision, standing there with Lady Bethune gazing at me intently. Though I was not comfortable with it, in this case discretion seemed the better part of valor. I would not tell the innkeepers the truth about my purse, that I no longer had the ability to pay for the room and the service I would need. I would wait until Ty was well and say nothing about the state of my finances until then. Only time would tell if this was a wise decision, but right or wrong, I felt it was the *only* one, the expedient thing to do in terms of Ty's well-being.

When Mrs. Brindle came out of the kitchen, bringing another pot of coffee, I beckoned her over. "My brother's fever is still high, his breathing worse; I fear we cannot continue our journey. Could you send for a doctor? I would feel so much better if I had him looked at by a physician."

"The poor little tyke is worse then?" She seemed genuinely concerned. I thanked God that this unlucky twist of fate at least had brought us to an inn kept by someone as understanding as she appeared to be. How misleading appearances can be I was not to find out until later. I myself was trying to protect the appearance of a well-born lady acting in a proper manner given difficult circumstances. It seemed to work. Mrs. Brindle immediately offered to summon the local doctor.

"Dr. Hardin lives not a stone's throw from here. He always stops here for a morning coffee, either on his way out to make sick calls or on his way back from an all-night delivery, as the case may be. I'll send him right up."

I thanked her and started to turn away.

"Don't you want a bit to eat, miss? Nursing takes all your strength."

"I should get back upstairs. I asked your maid to stay with Ty while I spoke with you—" I hesitated.

"At least, have some good, hot tea. Here, let me pour you a mug to take up with you. I'll send Peg up with a tray of food so you can have it while you wait for the doctor."

"That's very kind of you. Thank you." I gratefully took the mug she handed me. The tea was strong and sweet. As I took a sip and felt its warming strength flow through me, Lady Bethune got up from her place and moved slowly toward me.

"The child is ill?" she demanded. "You won't be continuing on with us then?"

"Ty has a bad cold and isn't up to traveling. No, we won't be going."

"What about your relatives, the ones you said were expecting you? Won't they be waiting at the stagecoach station for you?" Her high-arched eyebrows drew together over curious eyes. "I could take a message, telling the reason for your delay."

"That's very kind of you, Lady Bethune," I began, touched by such unexpected thoughtfulness on her part. Then caution checked me.

I had no assurance that the Hazeltons knew we were coming. Maybe they had not received the note I'd posted before I left school. Worse still, by this time Muir might have found out that Ty was not going to Nanny's sister's, but that *I* had taken him. If that had happened, Muir might already have contacted the Hazeltons, threatened them, reminding them of his legal rights. By what little I knew of the courts, I was afraid Muir would win any custody dispute. Even worse, what if Muir gained knowledge of our whereabouts, came after us, and forcibly took Ty?

I decided I best not give out any more information.

"That won't be necessary, but thank you," I said, my voice cooler than I intended because of my own fear.

She shrugged. "As you please. I know I would be upset if I were expecting two young people I cared about to arrive and they didn't show up. Word of our accident has most probably already gone out. Bad news always travels fast, wrong accounts even faster. They might be saying by now there were no survivors, that all of us perished instead of crawling out of an overturned coach like scurrying monkeys." She sniffed and started back to the table.

I hoped I had not offended her by my refusal. She turned around and, frowning, asked again, "You're sure?"

"Yes, but thank you very much."

She shrugged and went back to the table and took her seat beside Thompson. I saw her say something to her maid, who glanced my way. I assumed they were discussing me. I was sure they thought me rather odd, but they knew only part of my circumstances.

I set down the mug and went back to the stairway. Halfway up I heard the driver's loud voice announce, "We're ready to load up, folks. All going to Dorset!"

Although their possessions had not been retrieved, the other passengers had decided to continue on their journey. The driver had assured us that as soon as the rain stopped men would dive to find and bring up the luggage that had plummeted into the water when the coach overturned. The stage company would contact the owners so they could identify and claim their salvaged belongings. My trunk and Ty's trunk had either been swept downstream or had settled in the mud at the bottom of the swollen river.

How I longed for us to be on our way again to the haven of the Hazeltons' home. Every day Ty was away from Crossfield Grange intensified the danger of discovery. I was deathly afraid of Muir's actions should he find out what Nanny and I had conspired to do and then actually done.

From the window of our room I saw the stagecoach depart. As I watched it drive off and disappear around the bend of the road beyond the inn, a strange desolation overwhelmed me. The feeling of being friendless, forsaken, and destitute left me momentarily weak. I wished then I had at least given Lady Bethune the names and address of Aunt Evelyn and Uncle George. But it was too late, and the sensation of being truly alone with the responsibility of my sick brother became frighteningly real.

Resolutely, I put such thoughts from me. I must be strong, for Ty's sake. He was still asleep, tossing and mumbling feverishly. I knelt beside the bed, took his hot, little hand in my own, and prayed as I had never prayed before, for his recovery and for our continued protection and safety.

Within twenty minutes a doctor with a craggy, weather-beaten face and a bushy beard arrived to examine Ty. He was so cheerful and optimistic, my own low spirits lifted. He ordered poultices be placed on Ty's chest and a steaming kettle be kept nearby for vapor to keep his lungs from becoming congested. "Good nursing and a few days' rest should have him right as rain," Dr. Hardin assured me heartily.

Although Mrs. Brindle had been particularly solicitous about Ty, I worried constantly about her reaction when she found out the state of our financial situation. During Ty's illness she had sent up fresh linens and towels every day. Trays, too, for both of us as Ty began to take nourishment. All these services were rendered by an unwilling Peg, who made her reluctance to do this extra work evident. It seems the other maid was actually a village girl who came in to help only when the inn needed her.

As far as I could tell from what I overheard when downstairs, little had been recovered from the wreck. All the luggage on the top of the stage had toppled into the river, and most of that was ruined by water. All Ty and I had were the clothes we were wearing when we were rescued.

True to Dr. Hardin's prediction, a few days later Ty was better. Then came my moment of truth. I knew I could not put off telling the innkeepers about our predicament any longer.

That evening, after I'd finally gotten Ty settled in bed, I took courage and went downstairs. With all the forthrightness laced with gratitude I could manage, I haltingly explained my situation to the Brindles.

They stared at me, aghast, as I told them of my penniless state. Quickly their expressions changed from disbelief to indignation and finally to anger. Mrs. Brindle was quicker to react than her husband, who was in a besotted state.

Her eyes protruded, her face reddened, and her expression turned ugly. "Well, I must say, this is a fine state of affairs. Not only did I give you the best room in the inn, which rightly should have gone to her ladyship and her maid, but *you* insisted on special services besides. You've got a fair nerve, my girl! We should call the sheriff that's wot! Can't pay, eh? Well, we'll just see about that!"

"You have every right to be upset, Mrs. Brindle. Believe me, I understand. But it wasn't my fault my belongings, including the purse containing all my money, were lost in the stagecoach accident. All I could think of was taking care of my little brother." I swallowed hard, and attempting to appeal to their sympathy, added, "I am all he has in the world."

"Yes, well, be that as it may, remember we had the doctor up to see the lad—come out in all the storm, he did—and that's an extra charge." Mrs. Brindle pushed out her lower lip aggressively.

Her statement was not quite true, but I was in no position to argue. I merely nodded and went on. "I know. I much appreciated that, and I'm very grateful. Maybe it was wrong of me not to tell you right away about the money, but what else could I have done? Ty could not travel farther and—"

I paused, searching both faces for some understanding, some hope of kindness. I met with stony, blank faces. "I fully intend to pay you back for everything."

"Just how do you expect to do that, miss?" Her mouth twisted. "Have your fairy godmother wave a wand and magically bring all the money you owe us?"

"I will work it off. I'll do whatever you say until I've paid back every penny."

"*You!*" she scoffed. "What can you do with them lily-white, soft hands, them delicate bones?" Her narrowed eyes moved over me scornfully.

I drew myself up. I had to convince her. Visions of debtors' prison, Ty in an orphanage, rose in my fevered imagination. "I'm much stronger than I look."

Mrs. Brindle still looked skeptical. What more could I say to soften her? Had I been entirely mistaken about this woman? She had seemed so kind, at least about Ty. Of course, she *had* thought I was gentry, that she would be well recompensed for all her trouble.

She eyed me with cold contempt.

Swallowing my pride, I took another tack. "Mrs. Brindle, the stagecoach accident was no one's fault. I cannot help it if my brother and I are alone in the world. I have offered you a fair deal, I believe. I am willing to work off my indebtedness."

Mr. Brindle's bloodshot eyes made a slow, rather insolent appraisal of me, which brought the blood rushing into my face. Then for the first time he spoke. "She's got a point, Molly. I could use her in the taproom. I'm always shorthanded these nights, pertickerly Saturdays. She's surely strong enough to pull a pint, carry trays, serve customers, and wash up after closing."

Mrs. Brindle shot him a scathing look, but I could see she was considering his suggestion. She chewed her lower lip for a moment, gave me another long look. I felt like a horse at auction. It was humiliating to have them evaluate me as if I were livestock.

Then almost as if thinking out loud she said, "Well, she's pretty enough, I 'spect. We'll give it a try."

In another minute a bargain was struck. It was agreed that I would work as a general housemaid during the day and as a barmaid in the evenings when the taproom opened for business. Mrs. Brindle would figure out the total I owed for room, board, and services rendered.

From that moment I was treated as a servant. Mrs. Brindle had the last word and all the power in the situation, telling me that if my work wasn't satisfactory, there was still the possibility of turning us over to the authorities. Thus she cleverly hung over us, like the Sword of Damocles, the threat of debtors' prison, an orphanage, and, that of which she was not even aware, discovery by Muir and the very real possibility that he would take Ty away from me forever.

*S*o began a time in my life I would always look back on as something out of a nightmare. It took less than an hour for my new status to be known throughout the inn. Ty and I were removed from our comfortable room and sent to the attic, a cubbyhole under the eaves. The day after I confessed the truth to the Brindles I was handed a gray muslin dress, a rough, faded, blue cotton coverall to wear over it, and a calico scarf to tie over my head. My hair was to be braided and pinned up, Mrs. Brindle ordered, instead of falling in its natural waves to my shoulders. My high-heeled boots were replaced by sturdy clogs to be worn with heavy woolen stockings.

I, who had been brought up in luxury, waited upon and served, now found myself the lowest in the pecking order of the inn's staff of servants. I was immediately placed in the kitchen as the cook's helper and set to tasks for which I was completely unprepared—washing dishes and greasy platters, cleaning cooking pots and pans, scrubbing potatoes until my hands were raw, stirring stews in a steaming pot over a hearth fire.

It was a far cry from anything I had ever known. With virtually no experience, I had to be shown how to do everything, and I was awkward and clumsy. This made me the target of irritated tongue-lashings from the cook and the scullery maid.

After my morning chores in the kitchen, Mrs. Brindle sent me to help Peg clean the guest rooms, change the linens, and make the beds. Peg had been a rather sullen girl even when she thought I was a guest. Now she treated me with utter contempt. She seemed to take pleasure in assigning me the most odious jobs: emptying the slop jars, collecting the ashes in the fireplaces, dragging heavy baskets of used sheets down to the laundry shed and returning with heavier loads of ironed linens. I had to trundle the large brass vats downstairs and out to the well, fill them with water, and lug them back up to fill a washstand jug in each room.

Although I thought I'd mentally prepared myself for the physical work I would have to do to pay our debt, I was not prepared for the daily disgrace of being a servant. The staff members treated each other harshly. There was no gentleness, no tactful suggestions, no compliments on jobs well done, only name calling and ridicule. I never heard so much as a please or thank you. My sudden downfall to this lowly position made me the butt of rude jokes, the topic of coarse humor.

In the afternoon I put on a clean apron and head scarf and reported to Mr. Brindle behind the bar. I had to sweep and spread fresh straw on the floor before the place opened for business. By five o'clock, yeomen, farmers, millers, blacksmiths, and shopkeepers began to come in for their nightly convivial ale or spirits.

I may have been able to withstand the hard labor of the daytime work if it had not been for my assignment to the taproom at night. I found it the worst possible form of punishment, humiliating in the extreme. Worse still, after my exposure to Muir's abuse of spirits, and its ruinous effects on the lives of my mother and little brother, the thought of working in a place that dispensed it, as well as nightly being around people who consumed it, was repugnant to me. However, I had no choice but to comply with the terms of my agreement with the Brindles.

Weary as I was from my daily chores, the evening seemed endless. In the beginning I only washed tankards and mugs behind the bar, keeping Mr. Brindle supplied with clean ones as the press of crowd grew. Mr. Brindle often drank along with the customers, becoming less coherent, more blurred of eye and slurred of speech as the evening progressed. Within a week or so, he had me serving the tables. This I disliked as much as anything else I had to do.

Each night when the tavern finally closed at midnight, I climbed the steps to our attic room, almost in tears from weariness and exhaustion. The knowledge that this situation was only temporary kept me from giving in to despair.

As an early and useless bid for sympathy, and more importantly because I did not want the Brindles to contact Muir, I had told them that Ty and I were orphans, which in my case was true, and that we were on our way to our only relatives when the accident occurred. Most of the time I held back the fear that somehow Muir would find out where we were. Sometimes, however, I awoke in the middle of the night shaking from a bad dream in which he had found us.

I tried to put a brave face on our situation for Ty's sake. Using all my storytelling ability, I made our plight sound like one of the adventures I used to make up for him. I wove a tale that we, the prince and princess of a faraway kingdom, had been put under a spell and were being held captive, that we would have to plan and plot secretly our escape.

"You mean some witch has put a spell on us, Lyssa?"

"Something like that."

Completely caught up in this pretend game, Ty's eyes shone with excitement. "But we *will* find our way out some day, won't we?"

"Of course," I said, wishing I were as sure as I sounded.

His little brow puckered, then he asked, "Is Mrs. Brindle the witch?"

"Oh, Ty, don't ever let her hear you say that!" I was unable, in spite of our serious situation, to keep from laughing. "Actually, she's been kinder than we had any right to expect, likely kinder than most innkeepers would be. After all, I do owe her a lot of money. I'm working very hard to free us from the spell."

"I know. I will too, Lyssa." He looked serious. "I can feed the chickens and bring in the eggs for Cook."

I hugged him hard. "You're a champion, Ty!"

"Just maybe a prince from another country will come and rescue us like in *Briar Rose*. Do you think?"

I shook my head doubtfully. "I don't think so, Ty. I think we're going to have to work this out ourselves."

Though I had enjoyed reading fairy tales as a child, I'd never quite believed in the fairy-tale solution of a handsome knight on a white charger coming to save a fair damsel and take her away to live happily ever after. That had been too contrary to my experience of the *real* world.

All our hardships notwithstanding, at least Ty was well. In fact he was thriving. He had become the pet of the place. The cook had taken a fancy to him and saw that he got the best food. During the day he played with the cat and her kittens and helped in the vegetable garden. He was such an appealing child, merry and sweet natured, it would have been hard for anyone not to grow fond of him. I do believe *he* was the reason the other servants' attitudes toward me gradually improved.

This was true of all the servants—all except Peg, the overworked general housemaid. She was the one holdout not won over by Ty, but who could blame her after finding out that the *lady* who had demanded so much extra service—frequent hot water, clean linens, trays and extra pots of tea—was not only poor as a church mouse but, by deceiving the

Brindles, was also, in her opinion, no better than a common thief.

Her hostility was unrelenting. All my attempts at friendliness failed. She ridiculed me, pointed out my mistakes, made ugly, cutting remarks to me, and complained to Mrs. Brindle about me. I understood why she resented me. From birth our destinies were ordained to be different. My situation, no matter how low, was temporary, while Peg had been born into poverty, and with no education, her position would remain the same. I could not disguise my accent nor hide the fact that I had been used to another kind of life. No wonder Peg hated me.

Gradually our lives took on a sort of pattern. The account I was keeping of our indebtedness was steadily growing even. Soon I would be able to pay off the Brindles, and Ty and I would be free to leave and continue on our journey to Briarwood Manor.

I did not mind the hard work in the daytime but I greatly disliked working in the taproom in the evenings. There I had to ignore the ogles and remarks made to me or about me as I served. I kept telling myself it would soon be over. Soon this wretched experience would be a thing of the past.

Then one morning something happened that jolted me. As I was coming downstairs with a bundle of sheets piled in a willow basket, the front door of the inn burst open and a tall man, his dark cape billowing behind him, strode into the center of the room. The blustery wind caught the door, slamming it against the wall and making his entrance even more dramatic. Startled, I almost dropped the laundry, and Mrs. Brindle, standing behind the counter, turned around with a jerk.

He stood, looking around him, and from where I stood on the staircase I could see his face clearly. It was Lady Bethune's nephew, Nicholas Seymour! His heavy, dark brows drew together as his penetrating gaze met mine. Instinctively I drew back. While I recognized him immediately, I was sure he would never recognize the grubby maid I had become. He would never make the connection between the well-dressed young lady, his aunt's traveling companion, Miss Challys Winthrop, and a scruffy maid working at a country inn.

There was, however, an instant of hesitation as though he were about to take a step toward me or speak, but Mrs. Brindle, sensing a paying customer, bustled forward, all warmth and welcome. "Good day, sir. What can we do for you? A room for the night? Your horse stabled?"

Her tone of voice was noticeably different from the one she used toward the servants, far different from the one in which she usually addressed *me*.

Seymour turned toward the woman. "No, madam. Thank you very much." His voice was deep, authoritative. "I have come to inquire whether any of the belongings of the passengers on the stagecoach that met with the accident several weeks ago have been retrieved from the river? My aunt, Lady Bethune, was among the unfortunate travelers marooned here afterward. She is missing some very valuable belongings. I thought they might have been brought here for identification."

Mrs. Brindle seemed flustered, and afterward, when I thought about it, rather furtive and defensive in her manner. I passed it off at the time, thinking she was offended by Seymour's remark about "unfortunate travelers marooned here." "No, sir, none as I know of. What was brung up was done by a salvage company hired, I think, by the stagecoach line. I dunna heard of anything of value being found. It was a very stormy night indeed, the night of the accident. The current in the river is treacherous. Like as not most things was swept downstream."

"Well, then, that's that." Seymour brushed his hands together in a dismissive gesture. "Luckily, her maid held on to her jewel case containing most of the irreplaceable items, but since I was on my way to my aunt's for a visit, she requested I at least stop and inquire. Thank you, madam, and good day to you."

As he swung around to retrace his steps to the front door, he again glanced toward where I stood, trying to make myself invisible. He halted, and again our gazes met—I flattened myself against the wall, feeling heat rise into my face. He seemed to hesitate as he pulled on his leather gloves. For a few seconds he remained motionless, as if he were grasping at something that eluded him. He frowned, then giving his head an almost imperceptible shake, marched toward the door, yanked it open, and went out.

With the door's slam, I felt my tension ease, but in the next minute I felt a scalding resentment. Until I was in the position of a servant, I did not realize how people treated them. To Seymour I was no more than a part of the woodwork. Of course, I had not wanted him to recognize me. Still, I was determined that when I got out of my own bondage, I would be aware of those serving me and treat them kindly.

After Seymour's departure, to my surprise, Mrs. Brindle hurried to the window, peered out as if to make sure he had gone, then went to the cellar door and opened it. "Brindle!" she called. "Come up here at once! I got sumpin' to tell you."

I heard a muffled reply from below where Mr. Brindle was gathering stock for tonight's tavern trade from the wine cellar.

Mrs. Brindle stood there, hands on her hips, tapping her foot impatiently. "*Now,* I said, Brindle!"

Within minutes I heard the clump of boots and the rattle of glass as a red-faced, puffing Mr. Brindle emerged through the door behind the counter, carrying a wooden box of bottles. "Whatja want?"

I tried to slip down the rest of the steps and disappear out through the back hall to the laundry shed, but Mrs. Brindle turned and spotted me. "What are you gawkin' at? Gwan wi' your work."

I hurried past but not before I heard her say to her husband, "We got a bit of trouble, unless—"

Unless what? What kind of trouble did she mean? What, if anything, did it have to do with Nicholas Seymour's unexpected visit?

8

or the rest of the day I felt depressed. Seeing
Nicholas Seymour—handsome, well groomed, ex-
pensively dressed, assured of his position—made
my present situation doubly hard to bear. It was all I could
do to get on with my chores. My evening stint in the taproom
loomed, even larger than usual, and with it my other worries.

I should write Nanny Grace at her sister's address, where
she was supposed to be visiting with Ty, at least to let her
know where we were. Yet, how could I let Nanny Grace know
what had happened to us, especially with the Brindles
watching my every move, keeping me busy from sunrise to
sunset. And what if, having discovered Ty was gone, Muir
went after Nanny and threatened her? Having witnessed his
frightening rages, to be the target of one would be terrifying.
Letting Nanny know where we were might put her in greater
jeopardy. No, I couldn't take that chance. And I couldn't risk
the possibility of Muir finding us. What I'd done was criminal—kidnapping! Children were the property of their father.
I had taken Ty without Muir's permission, even his knowledge. He could drag me into court, have me thrown into
prison. A young woman like me would stand no chance

against a powerful man. I shuddered at the possibilities should Muir find us.

All these complicated thoughts churned in my mind as I entered the taproom to take up my duties that evening. To my disgust I found Brindle had been tippling earlier, even before the evening had begun. He was far into his cups.

He was flushed of face and slurred of speech, refilling his own glass whenever he filled one for a customer. At this rate he wouldn't last the evening. This was not a new occurrence. More than once I had been forced to summon Mrs. Brindle to help him to bed. Then I'd been left to clean and lock up on my own.

It was, as usual, crowded and noisy, and I was kept constantly on the go, clearing tables, serving round after round of drinks, picking up empties, and taking back refilled mugs. I'd learned, for the most part, to ignore the bold ogling, the coarse remarks, sometimes purposely made loudly enough for me to hear, as I moved about. Mentally, I gritted my teeth, repeating to myself, *This too shall pass.*

That night a frequent customer was there, one who was remarkably different from the regulars. I'm not sure when I first became aware of Francis Vaughn, but by the time he had come in several evenings in a row, I had noticed him.

He was young, boyish looking almost, with rounded features, a soft beard, and thick, curly, dark hair. He was slight of build, and he spoke in a low voice with an accent I couldn't place. The thing about him that stood out most to me was that he was always polite, thanking me when I served him, leaving an extra coin as a tip. The other unusual thing about him was that he brought a small sketchbook with him and spent the evening sketching the other patrons. One night I could not help but see a rendering he'd made of the village baker, a man with strong features and interesting facial expressions.

"That's very good," I said. I knew nothing of art, but it did seem to be somewhat of a good likeness from what I could tell.

"Only a quick impression." He shrugged, then he looked

up at me and said intently, "I'm an *artist*. My name is Francis Vaughn." He smiled. "Remember it. Some day I'm going to be very famous."

He sounded very sure of himself. Boastful, even. I started to move away, but he stopped me with a question. "What is someone with the face of an angel doing in a place like this?"

I must have looked startled, for immediately he apologized, saying, "Please don't be offended. It's just that I noticed you right away. The first time I came in here. As an artist, I'm always looking at people as possible models and naturally—maybe, you don't realize how—well, what an interesting face—I'd love to paint you."

He went on to tell me he was living near the village in a small cottage turned into a studio. He seemed eager to talk more, but just then an impatient customer banged his empty mug on the bar top, and I looked over my shoulder nervously. "I have to go."

"If you'd consent to pose—"

"Oh, I couldn't. I have no time."

"Not even one day a week?"

Mr. Brindle's loud voice reached me then, and I had to hurry off.

When I came by his table again, Vaughn ordered another drink and whispered, "If you would pose for me, I can pay you in a few days what it would take you a month to earn here as a serving girl." He went on to say he had received a commission for a special kind of portrait for a prestigious gentlemen's private club in London, but he had not found the right model yet.

By this time in the evening, the noise level had risen along with the amount of alcohol consumed. The crowded room was hot, filled with the smells of men who had come straight from field, forge, and barn, and loud with argumentative voices and the clatter of tankards against wooden tables. The heavy tobacco smoke from a dozen tar-encrusted pipes hung in the air. My head pounded, my feet hurt, my back ached. Anything that promised escape from this nightly scene would have sounded tempting, but I hesitated. "Think about it, will you?" Vaughn persisted as he pressed a piece of paper into my hand.

The rest of the night I did not have much time to think. Mr. Brindle was hardly any help, huddled in one corner of the bar with two unsavory-looking fellows whom I did not recognize as regulars. I had to fill the pint-sized beer mugs myself, as well as collect the empties and wipe off the counter.

I reminded him when it was time to close. To my surprise he waved me off, telling me I could leave, that he'd shut down the place. He was still with the two men I'd noticed earlier. Well, it was nothing to me. Mr. Brindle would have to answer to his wife.

Wearily, I plodded up the steps, ready to fling myself on the lumpy mattress for a few short hours of sleep. As I undressed, I found the slip of paper in my apron pocket that Vaughn had given me. I took it out and read it. In a distinctive, curling hand he'd written the directions to his studio-cottage and the hourly rate for modeling. He was right. It was more than I made here in a day.

I got into bed and pulled the thin blanket over my shoulders. Every muscle twitched from fatigue. Anything would be better than what I was doing. I had discovered that barmaids were notoriously underpaid. Although allowed to keep whatever tips customers left, I could see it would be slow going indeed to pay back the amount Mrs. Brindle figured we owed her. All the "extras" we had enjoyed when Ty was ill had added up to a tidy sum. If I could hasten our leaving even by a few days, wouldn't it be worth it?

But could I trust Francis Vaughn? Artists were not really respectable. Except, of course, for those whose work was hung in the Royal Gallery. What did I really know of Vaughn?

I closed my eyes and was soon asleep. Vaughn's offer, then,

might have just as easily been forgotten except for two un-foreseen events.

As I said, the cook had become fond of my little brother, though I did not know how fond until the fair came to the village and she gave me time off to take him. I was surprised that morning when instead of giving me my orders for the day she provided me with the excuse to give Mrs. Brindle. Besides the carnival attractions—clowns, magicians, and puppet shows—local farmers set up booths to sell their produce of vegetables, fruit, and specialties of all sorts. The cook handed me a list of items to bring back, adding gruffly, "No need to hurry. Give the lad a chance for a treat and a ride or two."

I realized she was doing this from a heart recently thawed by a little boy's smiles. Nonetheless, I appreciated the chance for a day off, and so with a feeling of freedom I had not experienced for weeks, Ty and I took off for the village.

Even before we saw the bright tents and flapping flags, we heard calliope music and the sounds of a large crowd. The nearer we got to the village the more chaotic the scene around us became. Everyone seemed to be going to the fair. People on foot, in carts, carriages, and coaches, as well as riders on horseback, added to the confusion. The noise of shouts and laughter grew louder. Holding Ty's hand, I quickened our pace, a sense of anticipation mounting with every step.

We passed through the entrance, jostled on every side by people. The holiday air was contagious. Ty gave a little skip and, swinging my hand back and forth, asked excitedly, "What shall we do first, Lyssa?"

"Let's take a look all around, then decide." Besides the money the cook had given me, I'd brought along a few coins of my own from tips earned in the taproom. I'd squirreled them away without guilt, given, as they were, directly to me. Now was the perfect time to use some of them. I'd have to account for the cook's purchases when we got back, and the little extra money she'd given us did not amount to much. But I wanted Ty to have a good time. The poor little fellow had been so good and patient all this time with no playmates and only the small kitchen yard in which to roam, not to mention the long evenings he had to spend alone upstairs while I worked in the taproom. I wanted him to have at least this one day of fun. Still I'd have to be careful and pick and choose how to spend our tiny amount.

We wandered through the tented fairgrounds thronged with people. Everywhere there was color, movement. The midway was lined with booths of all kinds on every side, the owners hawking their wares. Booths decorated with streamers boasted baskets of rosy apples, golden pears, pumpkins, dark, leafy, green vegetables, bright orange carrots, and striped turban squash. Most of the sellers were pleasant, cheerfully greeting potential customers. Vendors sang out from wheeled wagons as they sold hot chestnuts, candied apples, fruit tarts, and sausages on buns.

The whole scene was such a direct and pleasant contrast with our grim existence that I was soon caught up in the merriment all around me. My one nagging wish was that we could somehow get lost in this crowd, slip away, and escape from our dreary serfdom to the Brindles.

It was then I saw Francis Vaughn.

He was sitting on a canvas stool outside a small tent in front of an easel. Before him in another chair sat a weathered-faced fisherman with a woolen cap pulled around large ears, red with cold. His blue eyes twinkled as he drew on a long-stemmed pipe. A plump woman with wispy gray hair stood nearby nodding approvingly. Vaughn was busy with his paintbrush, working steadily on the old man's portrait.

A sign nearby read, PORTRAITS, 1 shilling.

Almost at the same moment I saw him, he looked up and saw me. He smiled and beckoned me, his hand still holding the brush. I moved around behind him to see the small canvas propped on the easel. To me it looked like a good drawing, at least the cap and pipe were well rendered.

"That's very good!" I declared, nodding to the couple who beamed happily.

Vaughn worked swiftly and, with a few more strokes, signed his initials with a flourish at the bottom left side and handed the picture to the woman. She, in turn, counted out the fee into his outstretched palm.

"Next?" Vaughn said hopefully, turning to me.

"Oh, no." I shook my head. "We're here to have fun."

"Don't turn me down. I'll do one of your brother here free if *you* will sit for me. I've been wanting to sketch you since I first saw you." He snapped his fingers. "I've got an idea. Your brother can ride the carousel while you pose. It's right over there." He pointed to the gaily painted merry-go-round a few yards away. "You can keep your eye on him while you pose for me."

"Oh, please, do say yes, Lyssa," Ty begged. "Can I?"

"*May* I." To Vaughn I said, "I don't know—"

"I'll be fine, *really,* Lyssa!" Ty tugged at my arm. "You can see me from here." He hopped from one foot to the other in his eagerness.

"Smart lad! Of course you'll be fine. Here's the price of two rides." Vaughn handed him a fistful of change.

Before I could protest, Ty was off and running toward the carousel.

"Take a seat, turn your head just so. I'd like a profile first." Vaughn began sharpening his charcoal stick.

It was a joy to see Ty having such a good time, and almost without thinking, I turned my head this way and that as Vaughn made several sketches. He made little murmuring sounds as he worked. The sound of the calliope lulled me, and Ty's smiling face and excited wave each time he came around on the merry-go-round made me glad. Strangely enough, I didn't even examine Vaughn's sketches. I was just happy to be free, at least for a while.

When his two rides were over, Ty came running back. We wanted to explore still other parts of the fair before we had to return to the inn, and Vaughn decided to close up shop and accompany us. As we wandered about, stopping at this booth and that, he told me more about himself. Although he was rather mysterious about it, he hinted that he had a famous London artist as a mentor. In fact, it was one of this artist's wealthy patrons who had lent Vaughn his weekend cottage outside the village. The man had seen some of Vaughn's work and had given him a commission as well as a place to paint. It was a great opportunity for a struggling artist.

"My dream, of course, is to have my work hung in the Royal Academy exhibit. You have to be really good; however, it doesn't hurt to have connections, people in high places within artistic circles to promote you."

We stopped, and Vaughn bought us all meat pies and cups of sweet cider. We sat on one of the benches in the little park set aside for picnickers.

"What I have in mind—that is, if you would consent to pose for me—is something like I've seen in the works of Millais and Rossetti. My patron is a great admirer of the Pre-Raphaelite painters."

"Pre-Raphaelite?"

"They were a group of idealistic artists that specialized in painting religious and allegorical themes. When I said you had the face of an angel, I meant that literally. You would be perfect for a painting I have in mind."

"But wouldn't such a painting take ages and ages?"

"It would take only three or four sittings. As you can see, I work quickly. And you would only have to pose for the face and figure. The background and details can be painted in afterward. As I told you, I can pay you very well. I already have a commission for the painting, and my commissioner is willing to pay the expense of a model."

"To tell you the truth, I don't think I'll be here much longer," I said, then, in a burst of confidence, I told him about the accident, Ty's illness, and our delayed journey to the home of our relatives.

"So you see, I have no time of my own. I must pay off our debt so we can be on our way."

"You'd get the money much faster, be on your way sooner, if you'd pose for this painting. Surely you can get off for a few hours on a Sunday?"

I thought that over. Mrs. Brindle reluctantly let her help off to attend services on Sundays. Since the taproom was closed on that day as well, there was very little to be done at the inn. Ty usually became restless during the church service. Only my promise of some special treat afterward made it bearable for him to sit still that long. If the weather permitted, that meant a picnic. If the cook was in a good mood, she let us pack a few apples, some cheese and bread, for our lunch. Maybe I *could* combine one of our outings with a few hours' posing for Vaughn.

Since I still had Cook's list of purchases to buy, I told Vaughn we needed to get going. We got up to leave.

"Think about it, won't you?" Vaughn urged.

"Yes, I will," I replied, not at all sure I would. I promised to let him know, and we parted.

When I think back on that afternoon, it all seemed friendly and harmless enough. Yet, as life so often teaches us, the things that cause the most trouble, those that bring the most regret, often start innocently.

9

*F*rancis Vaughn's offer the day of the village fair soon faded from my memory. Although Mrs. Brindle was supposedly keeping an account of what I was earning against what I owed, I kept my own tabulation. My tips each night were accumulating. I'd discovered the key to getting generous ones—being pleasant when I didn't feel like it, smiling when I'd rather frown. The sad truth was that the later it got and the more ale that was consumed the better the tips became.

We had been at the inn nearly two months by the time I figured we had enough to pay back the Brindles in full. We would need some additional money for our travel expenses. A couple weeks longer and we would be free. Knowing my days in bondage were nearing an end, I worked with more energy than ever.

I told Ty we would soon be leaving. Of course, since he did not have any of the same happy memories of Briarwood Manor that I did, he expressed mixed feelings at my announcement.

"I'll be sorry to leave Cook," he said doubtfully. "Tabby too." Tabby was the barnyard cat he had made his special pet. "She's just had kittens, just begun to let me handle them."

"But, Ty, I'm sure Auntie and Uncle George will let you have your own cat and a dog, if you like, probably even a pony. I did when I was a little girl and lived with them at Briarwood."

That seemed to encourage him, and he entered into my plans more enthusiastically.

The night before I planned to leave, I laid out our clothes for travel. Ty had shot up like the proverbial weed over the last two months and had outgrown the things he'd worn on our journey. I was grateful Cook had passed along some clothes that had belonged to her numerous nephews. My one outfit, water stained and spotted from that night, was all I had. I cleaned and brushed it, made it as presentable as possible. I had not dared buy anything for either of us in the village, not even new ribbons for my poor battered bonnet. Knowing how the smallest scrap of gossip in a small town flies, I didn't want to risk having Mrs. Brindle confront me as to how I could spend any money when I hadn't paid her back. Better that we go as we were, even if we looked rather shabby.

The following morning I rose before dawn and dressed before waking Ty. My heart thumped anxiously. I didn't relish the encounter with Mrs. Brindle, even though it would be my last. I helped Ty with buttons and lacers, and we started down the attic steps.

To my dismay we met Peg coming up from the kitchen. Her mouth dropped open in surprise when she saw us.

"Wheredja think yer goin' dressed up like that?" she demanded. "You should have taken out the slop jars and fetched hot water afore this. We have two new lodgers, ya know."

I let go of Ty's hand and very deliberately drew on my gloves, carefully smoothing each finger. "Not *this* morning, Peg. Not *any* morning after this."

Her pale green gooseberry eyes popped wide, and the look on her face would have made me laugh if I hadn't been so nervous. Before she could regain either wit or tongue, I brushed by her with Ty in tow.

However, once we'd passed she leaned over the banister and shrilled, "Jest you wait till the missus hears about this!"

I didn't have to wait long. Mrs. Brindle evidently had heard our voices and was waiting at the foot of the staircase. Her startled expression turned to outrage when she saw us dressed for traveling.

"And what's all this about? Leaving you say? Without no notice. After all we done for you?"

"You must have realized we would be on our way as soon as I paid back the money I owed you, Mrs. Brindle."

"What makes you think you done that?"

"I've kept track of all I owed and the amount of work I've done. It tallies." I took out my ledger page and showed her.

"Wait jest one minute, miss high and mighty," she said after studying it. "I don't see any for the room you've been occupying and for the meals you've been eating since you started working off your first bill." She looked at me with narrowed eyes, her arms folded belligerently.

I was stunned. Surely she didn't expect payment for our miserable room and the skimpy meals we'd eaten?

"Did you expect charity after trying to cheat us out of what was our due when your brother was sick and we did all we could for you?" Her chin jutted out. "No, miss, not so fast. You still owe me." With a great show she turned the ledger around and started checking my figures. "The way I figure it, you still owe us two months of labor."

I bit back the words I felt like flinging at her. I felt Ty's hand tightening in mine. I knew I could not fight this. Mrs. Brindle had the upper hand. She could still make a case for the authorities if she had in mind to do so. If the sheriff were called, he might investigate, discover Ty and I had run away from Muir, and send Ty back. Furious but defeated, there was nothing I could do but agree either to pay the added amount, which I didn't have, or work it off.

For one rash moment I was tempted to pull out the chamois bag containing Mama's sapphire set that I had kept hidden beneath my mattress all this time and cast it into Mrs. Brindle's sneering face. It would more than pay our "ransom." But good sense prevailed. I would not waste my precious inheritance on such an unworthy cause. It would be like the biblical equivalent of selling my birthright for a mess of porridge. No, my mother's wish had been that I keep the jewels to protect my future, to sell them only as a last resort. This was not the emergency she had feared. I was young, strong, and healthy. As long as I could work, I would do what was necessary to settle this debt on my own.

With dragging feet, Ty and I remounted the stairs. Peg stood sneering on the landing as we reached it. I knew she had listened to every word of my confrontation with Mrs. Brindle. As we went past her, she hissed something vicious, but I ignored her.

"Never mind, Ty," I said as soon as we were in our room. "It will be all right. You'll see. They can't keep us here forever. I'll pay what she says we owe, but after that, we'll go. Don't worry."

His trusting eyes wide, he nodded solemnly. I'd never felt the responsibility of my little brother more heavily.

That day all my chores seemed more onerous than ever. I couldn't believe I was still the Brindles' indentured servant. We'd been so close to freedom that this added sentence seemed unbearable. That night when I climbed the stairs to the attic, I felt completely worn out. As I wearily undressed, I caught a glimpse of myself in the cracked mirror above the washstand. Suddenly Francis Vaughn's request came back to me.

Holding my stub of a candle closer to get a better look, I studied my face. My high cheekbones were more prominent now that I had grown thinner. My eyes were large, long-lashed like Ty's, and like those of our mother. My mouth was rather full, my nose a little long. However, maybe to an artist, it seemed an interesting face to paint. I remembered the amount he said he would pay me for modeling.

Desperate times call for desperate measures, I had heard said. Now I realized just how desperate I was. After all these weeks I'd been slaving at the inn, I still owed the Brindles money, and I would need enough for the traveling expenses too.

The candle sputtered, then went out. I was left in the dark to grope my way over to the cot. How wonderful it would be when I no longer had to scrub another floor, clean another grease-caked pot, or serve another foaming pint of ale to a leering customer in the taproom.

Perhaps encountering Francis Vaughn was a stroke of luck, even the answer to prayer. Then and there I decided to tell Francis Vaughn I would pose for him.

The very next evening Vaughn came to the taproom. When I brought him his lager, I told him of my decision. Delighted, he started to tell me how to get to his studio-cottage. "I still have the directions you gave me," I whispered just as Mr. Brindle hollered from the bar, "Get a move on there, girl. There's customers waiting."

"I have to go," I said and hurried away to pick up another order. I was too busy the rest of the night to speak to Vaughn again, but before he left, he managed to slip me a piece of paper on which he had written "Sunday afternoon. FV."

Of course, Ty had to be in on our secret. He was excited. He remembered Francis from the fair and thought he was a "jolly fellow." Always game, my little brother made it sound like a great adventure.

The next Sunday, using the directions Vaughn had given me, we turned down a crooked road just before getting to the village, then followed a winding path to a fenced cottage nestled under leafy oaks. The cottage had a sloping thatch roof, diamond-paned windows, and a flagstone walkway leading to its red-painted door. It was actually quite charming, I thought as I knocked.

Vaughn opened the door almost immediately and greeted us enthusiastically. He ushered us into the large front room, a parlor, one end of which he had made into a studio. The canvas was concealed on a large, cloth-draped easel. Vaughn said he would incorporate some of the sketches he'd made of me at the fair with some full-length poses he'd make today. That was his method of working, starting with sketches and shifting to an oil painting later.

He said he was planning this composition in an Oriental style, much the fashion among artists just then, with a Chinese screen, perhaps, as background.

"May I see what you've done so far?" I asked, filled with curiosity.

He shook his head. "I never show a work in progress." His eyes twinkled mischievously. "You'll see it when it's hung in the Royal Academy exhibit."

He refused to answer my questions about the mysterious person who had commissioned the painting.

"I can say this, however. I've discussed my idea for this particular painting with my mentor, and he thinks it's fine. Now, it's time I gave you the tea I promised." He smiled.

Francis turned out to be a lively if rather clumsy host, dropping napkins, sloshing into our saucers the tea he poured from a brown, earthen pot. The tea was hot and fragrant, and we toasted crumpets on long forks over an open fire he'd built in the small fireplace. I remember the coziness of that Sunday afternoon, in sharp contrast to the gloomy weather outside.

After we'd had our tea, Vaughn found a box of old tin soldiers somewhere and a wooden Noah's ark with a menagerie of little animals. Ty was kept happily occupied while I posed.

"Will you paint me in this?" I asked, looking down at the dress I wore under my coverall as a maid.

"When I go up to London next I'll go to a costumer's and select something. It won't matter for now. Here—" he flung a length of Prussian blue material around my shoulders and arranged it. "This will do, the color is all I want to get. Loosen your hair. Let it fall—thus. Wonderful!" Vaughn seemed elated, high spirited that day.

He seated me on a high stool a few feet from his easel. It was my first such experience, other than that brief time at the fair, and I soon grew tired and stiff. My muscles ached from holding the pose. Francis, however, worked feverishly. I could hear the scrape of his brush on the rough fabric of the canvas. He seemed almost to forget me until I cleared my throat a couple of times and reminded him it was getting dark and I must get back to the inn.

Afterward, when I protested the amount of money he pressed into my hand, Francis assured me, "Money means nothing to the man who commissioned this painting. You've earned it."

He walked through the woods back to the road with us. "Will you come next week?"

"Yes." I said. "Same time?"

"Wonderful." He smiled.

As it turned out, I posed only a few more times for him—four Sunday afternoons out of a lifetime. Yet those hours were to have profound effects on both our lives.

10

*I*t was a strange interlude, a drastic change from my workaday week. The cottage tucked into the dense woodland seemed a world set apart. Francis Vaughn was like no one I'd ever met before. He matched the image I'd held of artists, meteoric and moody by turns, sometimes talkative, other times morose. I came to accept his erratic personality, though I never knew how he would be when I arrived. Sometimes silent, other times he talked constantly as he painted. Those times he seemed angry, speaking bitterly about less talented fellow students at art school who had connections. He criticized artists whose names even I recognized, saying they were unfairly elevated in the art world. Often he declared confidently, almost arrogantly, his assured future success.

"One day I *will* be well known, have clients clamoring for me to paint their portraits," he told me.

I simply listened, not always too attentively, my mind preoccupied as it was with my dilemma.

I do remember one particular day, though, when I found him quite depressed. He said he had wakened with a screaming headache brought on by a recurrent nightmare, and had been sleepless the rest of the night. He had a glass of wine in his hand as he let me into the cottage and offered me one from the half-full bottle on a table near his easel. I refused and said I should leave, that he probably did not feel like painting.

But he would have none of it. "I want to paint, I *need* to because—you see *that* is the nightmare. I dream I'm paralyzed somehow and can never paint again. I have lost the inspiration, the talent."

"Has this happened before?" I asked, feeling rather uneasy.

"It used to happen a lot. Before I met the man I told you about who sees my potential." Vaughn took a long sip of his wine.

"It all goes back to my childhood," he explained. His father, a once prominent merchant who had not encouraged his son in his art, had later been thrown into debtors' prison. Vaughn was plagued with the horror of suffering a like fate and with terrible guilt because he had not gone into business with his father and perhaps could have helped him avoid failure.

"I have to succeed," he told me fiercely. "I don't want you to go. You pose, I'll paint. If I'm alone, I'll drink too much."

I had seen him at the tavern a few times when I thought he'd had too much to drink, so I reluctantly consented to stay that afternoon. Things went all right, although Vaughn continued to talk erratically, the large onyx signet ring on his little finger flashing as he waved his hand about to emphasize some point he was making. I was shocked to hear that in the past, in times of deep depression, he had taken chloral, a powerful drug, to induce sleep so he could shut out his demons.

"I don't anymore," he said. "I *know* if I keep at it I *will* succeed. Now, someone believes in me."

Francis told me he would be going up to London the next day to show the preliminary sketches for the painting to his patron. I suppose I should have been more curious about this wealthy man to whom the cottage belonged and who was sponsoring Francis. However, my mind was usually preoccupied with other concerns.

While I sat modeling, I daydreamed of how wonderful it would be when Ty and I were at last at Briarwood Manor, safe and secure. It was then that I thought of a solution to my constant worry that no one knew where we were or of our sorry plight. When finally Francis said we were finished for the day, I got down from the stool on which I was perched and asked, "Francis, may I have some paper and the use of a pen? I'd like to write a note to my relatives who are expecting Ty and me and tell them of our delay."

"Of course," said Francis. He tore off a sheet of paper from one of his sketchbooks and handed it to me. I scribbled off a hasty note with only the merest of explanations. It was time to get back to the inn. Hurriedly, I folded it, addressed it, and handed it to Francis.

He glanced at it then raised his eyebrows and exclaimed, *"Lord and Lady Hazelton of Briarwood Manor* are your relatives?" He seemed impressed. "No wonder. I had an *uncanny* feeling about you. I knew you didn't belong in the Brindles' tavern." He paused, regarding me curiously. "These people are your relatives and you're working as a barmaid in a place like that?"

"It's a long story," I said quickly, wondering if I'd already revealed too much. "Too complicated to go into right now." I looked over at Ty, then said, "We must really get back. Come along, Ty."

Francis pocketed the letter in his smock, saying, "Not to worry. I'll take care this reaches its right destination."

The next Sunday Vaughn greeted me with unusual joviality. "I have some exciting news," he declared. My commissioner has seen the sketches, and he is very pleased. He especially likes the model!" He laughed. "His very words were, 'What a stunner,' so you can see, it all looks very promising."

"May I see the painting?" I asked.

"Not yet. I still have some final touches. But you have been very patient, and I'm grateful."

At the end of the session, Vaughn seemed particularly pleased with his afternoon's work. He still wouldn't let me see the painting, but he did press an extra coin into my hand as Ty and I were ready to leave, waving away my protest. "Actually, your part is finished, though I hope you will pose for me again. I have another idea in mind for which you'd be the perfect model."

"I doubt it, Francis. You have helped me enormously with this payment. But I will be leaving—very soon." I stopped, wondering how much I should confide in him. No one from the inn knew where we spent Sunday afternoons, nor of my association with the artist, and he had been warm and helpful, providing me with an unexpected windfall of cash. "This has helped me pay off our debt, and I'm very grateful. I hope we can soon leave for my relatives'."

He frowned. "I don't understand why you didn't contact them right away. Surely they would have sent you money, being who they are. Members of the aristocracy and all."

Quickly I explained that Lord and Lady Hazelton were elderly and I did not want to distress them. I held up the money he had just given me. "With this, we should be on our way much sooner. Thank you."

"We shall *all* soon be very well off. Both of us freed of our shackles of poverty," he said grandly, giving me a conspiratorial wink. "This painting will make me famous. I feel it."

Mondays were always busy in the taproom. Men deprived of their pints with their fellows on Sunday swarmed into the tavern early, drank heartily and long. Brindle not the least. I gathered he spent most Sundays in solitary drinking. He certainly opened the taproom on Mondays somewhat the worse for his Sunday indulgence.

The same rough-looking men I'd seen him huddled with before showed up, and again the three of them went to a table at the far end of the room, leaving me to tend bar. It was a job I detested. As we were doing a brisk business I soon noticed the supply was getting low, the shelves of bottled spirits emptying rapidly.

Finally, I went over to Mr. Brindle and whispered, "Excuse me, sir."

He turned around, obviously annoyed at being interrupted. When I told him the problem, he snarled, "Here, go down to the cellar and bring up a dozen or so bottles—the red."

He thrust his ring of keys at me. I stood there for a few seconds, holding them. He'd never before entrusted me on such an errand.

As I hesitated, he snapped, "Whatja waitin' for? Get a move on. Customers waitin'." He turned back to his companions and lowered his head, clearly continuing the conversation I'd interrupted.

I had to pass by the register counter, where Mrs. Brindle was nodding at her post. She gave a kind of snort as I went by but did not waken.

There were several keys on the ring, and I had no idea which one to use. I went down the narrow stone steps to the lower part of the house. When I reached the bottom of the stairway, I held the candle high and looked around. The space was circular, with three wooden doors. Which one led to the storage room for the tavern? They looked similar. I'd just have to try to find the right one.

Starting at my left, I tried one key, then another, but I couldn't get any to slide in or turn easily. I tried the second door and found a key that twisted slightly. I gave the key a push, and the door squeaked open. Raising the candle, I peered in.

It was a storage room, but not the one containing the wine. There were no shelves or barrels. It was hardly bigger than a pantry. Something caught my eye, however, and I stepped forward cautiously and slowly turned around. I saw a number of trunks and assorted luggage. There was even a wicker hamper, very much the worse for wear, dented, bent out of shape, its willow strips broken. I took another step in, tipping the candle to shine in front of me so I could get a better look.

Seeing something familiar, I crept closer. A small humpbacked trunk. When I bent nearer I saw it bore the initials CW on the metal plate below the lock. *My* trunk! The one I thought had been swept away when our stagecoach toppled into the river! My breath came shallowly as I glanced around. I recognized more articles. A now water-stained, expensive alligator tea kit. Wasn't it the one Lady Bethune's maid had carried? Had all these things been pulled from the wreckage? The very things Mrs. Brindle had assured Nicholas Seymour had *not* been recovered?

What were they doing stashed away under the inn? What were the Brindles up to? Were they selling these expensive items? Were they collaborating with thieves? I had thought the Brindles mean-spirited, conniving, and penny-pinching, but I had not thought them to be criminals. The two men I'd seen Brindle with in the tavern recently—*they* had the sly, dangerous look I would have suspected of crooks. Were they selling these stolen goods for the Brindles and then splitting the profits?

I began to shake. The candle in my shaking hand dripped hot wax on my skin, and I gasped. Were Ty and I literally trapped in a den of thieves?

Just then I heard heavy footsteps on the ceiling above. With a creak of hinges, the door to the basement opened, and Mrs. Brindle's voice bellowed down, "What's keeping you?"

Hastily, I backed out of the room, closing the door but not relocking it. "Coming!" I called back. "It's a heavy load."

I hurried to fit the next key on the ring into the lock on the third door. It opened easily. This was the wine cellar. I grabbed the nearest wooden box of wine bottles, lifted it, set it on the lowest step of the stairway, then shut and locked the wine cellar door behind me.

For the rest of the night, all I could think of was that room filled with my belongings and those of my fellow travelers. What should I do? Should I go to the authorities? Tell the Brindles I knew, confront them, threaten them? The thought made my knees weak, almost buckle. They wouldn't hesitate to accuse me of defrauding *them* and turn Ty and me over to the authorities who would possibly find out about Muir and notify him as to our whereabouts.

As I mechanically served drinks, washed mugs, and wiped counters and tables, my one compelling thought was that I must get Ty away from here before anything worse happened. Then I remembered Nanny Grace telling me she had sewn extra cash into the lining of Ty's trunk in case we should be delayed or need it on our journey. I hadn't seen Ty's trunk. I could only pray it was there. I had left the door to the storage room unlocked. Somehow I must go back down there before that was discovered, find the money, and take it. It was ours. Then Ty and I must escape.

It was difficult to work in the tavern the rest of that evening. I could think of nothing but the money sewn into the lining of Ty's little trunk, and how to get it without being caught. Should I even try on my own? What about all the other goods I had seen? Did the storage room contain items in addition to those belonging to the stagecoach passengers? Were the Brindles involved with thieves? Did the disreputable-looking fellows I'd seen whispering with Mr. Brindle bring their stolen goods here to be stored until they could be sold?

Every time I glanced at Mr. Brindle, a feeling of revulsion came over me. Maybe I *should* go to the town sheriff, tell him what I'd found. Let the law take care of it. But would they believe me? Might not my word be discounted as that of a disgruntled employee getting back at her employers? Wouldn't

I be accused of swindling the Brindles out of two months' room and board? I wished I had someone whose advice I could trust. But who?

Francis Vaughn? He was the only friend I had now. All evening I anxiously looked for him, hoping he'd come into the tavern, but he didn't show up. I decided to go over to his studio and tell him what I'd discovered. Maybe he could help me decide what I should do.

Usually I had about an hour late in the afternoon when I was supposed to wash up and change my apron and head scarf to prepare for my work in the taproom that evening. The following afternoon I hurriedly washed and changed, then slipped out the back door and ran practically all the way to Francis's cottage.

When he opened the door, he had a half-full wineglass in his hand. "Lyssa!" he exclaimed. "What a surprise."

"Francis, I need to talk to you."

"Come in."

Noticing he was dressed in a coat, wearing a shirt and cravat, I asked in dismay, "Are you going somewhere?"

"I'm going to London for a couple days." He seemed especially cheerful. "But there's time. What's the matter?"

As I stepped inside I saw a large, square package wrapped in brown paper and tied with string propped against the wall.

He saw my glance. "I've finished your painting, and I'm taking it to London to show my mentor and commissioner, then to have it framed."

"I haven't even seen it!" I exclaimed. Disappointment momentarily distracted me.

"I had a real inspiration about the background and worked round the clock to complete it." He smiled. "I've called it 'Lovers' Farewell.' You'll see it when it's on display in the Royal Academy."

All that seemed unimportant compared to my frightening discovery, the dreadful knowledge I now carried like a heavy stone. I poured out my story while Francis listened. By the time I finished, I was trembling.

He went to the cupboard for another glass, poured wine into it, and handed it to me. "Poor girl. You've had a dreadful shock. Here. Drink this."

I waved it away, shaking my head. "No. But, Francis, what should I do?"

"Nothing," he said flatly. "Unless you want to be tarred with the same stick. Accepting stolen goods is a crime. Knowledge is a crime. Concealing it could make you an accessory. The Brindles would probably twist the whole thing around so *you* would get into trouble. The police might even suspect you of being an accomplice." He took a long sip of wine. "If I were you, I'd say nothing. Get you and your brother out of there as fast as you can."

"But *my* things are among them. I could identify them."

Vaughn shrugged. "Then do as you like. I'm only giving you my opinion. They're a bad lot up there at the inn." He put down his glass. "I'm truly sorry I can't be of more help, Lyssa. I have to go or I'll miss the stage. My commissioner's expecting me for a celebration dinner at his club. I really must go."

"Of course." Obviously Vaughn was more concerned with his own affairs than he was with mine.

I went to the door; he followed.

"Take care. Don't do anything foolish."

Dejectedly I hurried back along the woodland path, the shortcut Francis had showed me, to the inn. I dreaded the night ahead more than ever. The discovery I'd made was dangerous. It had put Ty and me in even greater jeopardy. I had hoped for help from Francis Vaughn and had been disappointed. If the Brindles ever found out I knew—my heart jumped wildly.

11

*A*fter my discovery, working alongside Mr. Brindle in the taproom the next few nights was the hardest thing I'd ever done. Knowing what I now knew and seeing no possible solution, every time I glanced at his beady eyes, his rum-flushed face, I had to fight to keep from shuddering.

The Brindles were not only hard and unforgiving, eking out the pound of flesh for what I owed them, they were involved in criminal dealings. Vaughn's advice was right. We had to get away. We *had* to.

As I went about serving, wiping tables, picking up mugs, taking orders, I asked myself *how* I would manage it. I'd have to wait until the middle of the night when the household was asleep, slip down to the storage room, open Ty's trunk, if it was even there, and find the money Nanny had hidden. Then I would look for my own things, take whatever I could carry, and quietly sneak back upstairs. With the money from Ty's trunk, I would have more than enough money to pay back the Brindles in full and pay our travel expenses.

Toward the end of the evening Brindle was well on his way to being drunk, stumbling behind the bar, eyes at half-mast, tongue thick. When his attention was elsewhere, I took the knife with a sharp blade, the one Brindle used to slit the cork hood off wine bottles, a candle, and some matches. I slipped them into my apron pocket.

Just thinking about the possible repercussions of being caught set my heart thudding like a wooden clapper. A terrible inner debate ensued. Mr. Brindle was getting loud and argumentative with one of the customers, and Mrs. Brindle came in once or twice to check on him. This made me uneasy. Nothing escaped her eagle eye. A missing knife, a candle, would be spotted. Luck was with me, however. At closing time Mr. Brindle was head down on folded arms at the end of the bar. Mrs. Brindle marched in and, while berating him, half dragged, half pushed him out of the taproom and down the hallway to their room back of the lobby. Over her shoulder she ordered me to clean and lock up.

This was my chance. Alone, unwatched, I could slip down to the storage room. But I would have to be careful. The cellar door was behind the register counter at the front, which was *her* usual post, the spot where she remained until the tavern was closed. If she was busy putting Mr. Brindle to bed to sleep it off, she would be in their living quarters on the other side of the lobby. Still, the slightest noise might alert her and bring about my discovery. I remembered the squeaky hinges on the door to the cellar. I would have to take care of them. Some tallow or a bit of oil would do it—that is, if I waited another day. Perhaps I *should* wait another day. No. I couldn't afford to wait. I couldn't count on Mr. Brindle being this drunk again so soon. This might be the only night—my only chance.

I made as much noise as I could while cleaning up the taproom, shoving chairs on the tile floor, banging metal mugs, closing the shutters. I rattled the ring of keys loudly as I hung them on the hook behind the register. I let my heels clop on the steps as if I were on my way to the attic. At the bend of the stairway I crouched down, scarcely breathing, to wait until the house settled down for the night.

I don't know how long I sat there, hunched up, waiting. It seemed endless. I slipped off my clogs, crept down in my stocking feet, eased back along the wall until I was behind the register counter. My hand shook as I turned the knob of the door to the cellar.

I held my breath as I opened the door just enough so I could slip through. I bunched up my head scarf and thrust it between the door and its jam so the door couldn't bang shut and trap me. I felt along the wall for the worn, irregularly spaced steps leading down. I was afraid to light my candle until I got to the bottom.

Once there I took a long, shaky breath. My fingers searched my pocket and brought out the candle. I struck a match on the stone wall. My hand was shaking so much I didn't get the wick lit on the first attempt. The match burned my fingers, and I had to drop it.

"Oh, God, an ever present help in time of trouble. *Please!*" I prayed desperately.

I'd been taught not to presume on God's mercy if I did something reckless or took unnecessary risks. I knew I was doing something foolhardy and dangerous, but this was a matter of life and death, every bit as much for me as it had been for David when he was pursued by King Saul. Wasn't it? I fervently hoped so. I prayed as if it were.

My candle finally lit, the circle of light wavered as I started forward. Suddenly my mind went blank. I couldn't remember which door was which. Sweat formed in my palms, on my forehead, trickled down my back. Panic swept over me, and my whole body trembled.

Why hadn't I brought the keys with me, just in case? The thought of crawling back up the dark, twisting stairway, groping for the ring of keys, and making the descent again left me sick with fear. I desperately hoped the door was still unlocked.

Still praying, I took a few steps and pushed the flat of my hand on one of the doors. To my relief, it gave. I gulped as though I'd been drowning and just surfaced for air. I leaned my shoulder against the door and slowly it opened.

I would have to work fast. I did not know for sure how much time had passed since the taproom closed. If Ty and I were to get out of here, we would have to do it under cover of darkness. The Brindles would never let us leave otherwise. But now I couldn't think beyond finding the trunk and our money, then making it safely out of the cellar and back to the attic.

As long as I live I shall never forget those moments I searched frantically in the near dark for Ty's small, leather trunk. I hoped I could recognize it—if it was there at all. It might have floated away in the choppy river that stormy night. It had been one of the lightest, smallest objects. Still, I had to try to find it.

I felt like a beetle, scurrying around in the dark among the luggage, the odds and ends of bundles and boxes. I held the candle high. Its flickering flame shed only weak light. All I can now believe is that the Lord or my guardian angel guided me, for I was beginning to feel hopeless when, all at once, I saw Ty's little trunk. It was piled lopsidedly on top of a sagging willow basket in the corner behind a large gun case. I felt the stinging edge of tears as I scuttled over to the trunk. I tipped the candle, dripping some wax on the floor beside me, then stuck the end of the candle into the soft puddle so I would have both hands free. The trunk was wedged in so tightly, I had to work to shift heavier objects away so I could loosen it and pull it out. Luckily the lock had been broken by someone else in an attempt to open the trunk. When I lifted the lid, I saw that the once neatly packed clothes had been rumpled through, as if someone had been looking for valuables. Of course, such a cursory search would never have revealed a hidden cache of bank notes carefully sewn into the lining.

I reached for the knife. In my haste, I caught the sharp side of the blade. I drew in my breath as it cut into my flesh. Instinctively I stuck my finger into my mouth, sucking the blood the knife had drawn. Quickly I ran my other hand along the inside of the trunk. Under the lid I felt a ridge. The cloth gave easily. Soon I felt the reassuring thickness of a packet of notes. Thank goodness! The package was bound with ribbon. I thrust it into my apron pocket.

I made a quick job of investigating the whole interior lid, sides, and bottom, but found no more. After all, this had been taken from Nanny's own small savings. It was enough, I was sure, to get us on the stage and on our way to the Hazeltons—at last.

I had no sense of time. All I knew was that I was in a fearful race. I dared not think what would happen if I should be caught down here. My breath was coming fast and sharp. Once I was sure I had all the hidden money, I did not dare take the time to collect any belongings from my own trunk. Escape was more important. Ty and I must get away.

I retraced my steps quickly. Closing the door to the storage room, I thought again I should have brought the keys and relocked it. What would happen when the Brindles or one of their accomplices found it unlocked?

Well, I couldn't worry about that now. I had to get up the stairs and rouse Ty so we could get away before dawn broke.

*T*y, Ty! Wake up. There's a good boy." I shook him gently. He sat up, sleepily rubbing his eyes. His small mouth opened in what probably was a yawn, but afraid it might be a loudly voiced question, I quickly placed my hand over it. While he pushed at me indignantly, I whispered, "Listen, Ty, this is important. I'll explain later, but we have to leave *now,* without waking the Brindles or getting caught."

I leaned closer. "You must do exactly as I tell you and try not to make a sound. Promise?"

I felt his indrawn breath against my palm, and he nodded. I removed my hand. "Get dressed. Hurry."

There was not a minute to lose. Time wasted getting ready increased our danger of discovery. I got out of the despised maid's outfit and into the only other clothes I had, my traveling suit. I discarded my work clogs, but I kept on the heavy wool stockings. I tied my boots by their lacers to my waistband.

With Ty's help I wound the end of the sheet around the post of the bed and knotted it as hard as I could. We pushed the bed closer to the high dormer window on the slanted ceiling wall and pushed the window open. It had been driz-zling earlier, and the shingles would be slick. It would be difficult getting down to where the rain gutter ran along the edge of the roof, where we could drop to the ground. Dangerous, too, but we had to do it. I couldn't risk both of us stealing downstairs and out through the front door.

As agile as Ty was and as strong as I now was from the months of hard physical work, I felt we could make it. We *had* to. I knotted the thin blanket to the sheet and threaded it out through the window, letting it slide across the roof and dangle over the edge. There was still a good five-foot drop to the ground.

Should I go first, test the strength of the sheet and blanket, leave Ty to follow? Would it be safe to leave Ty in the room in case something went wrong, the sheet ripped, or I fell, or—I had to take the chance. He was a brave little fellow, but even so, it would be better to test my weight on the makeshift rope. If it held me, it would surely hold his much lighter body. Resentment at the thought of our stolen belongings stored downstairs along with those of other passengers drove my energy. But anger was a luxury I could not afford at the moment. I had to focus on our escape.

The packet of pound notes was my security, and I felt a curious satisfaction in having outwitted the thieves, who had not searched more thoroughly. I knew my self-satisfaction was probably wrong. I battled my conscience on this issue, but I felt no guilt for taking what was ours.

Even in my feverish haste to get away, I knew I had to take certain precautions. In their outrage at our departure, the Brindles might report us to the authorities, who would then be on the lookout for two fugitives on the road. I had to do my best to eliminate the possibility of pursuit. Therefore, I carefully counted out the money Mrs. Brindle said I still owed them and left it in plain sight on my empty cot. Although I doubted the amount to be true, I wanted to give them no reason to call us thieves.

Thrusting Mama's bag of jewels and our few other belongings into my shawl, I tied the ends together, knotting them securely.

"All right. We're set, Ty," I whispered. "Ready? I'll help you out, then you wait until I slide down and jump, then you come. When you jump, I'll be there to catch you. Can you manage?"

"Yes!" he said, his voice hoarse with suppressed excitement. For a lad his age, this was high adventure.

I lifted, shoved, and supported Ty as he climbed out the window, then I pushed our bundle of belongings through. Ty crouched outside the window on the slanted roof holding our bundle while I followed. It was much harder for me, with my skirt and larger body. I heaved myself up, squeezed through the narrow opening, and slid out, breathless and panting.

"You all right?" I asked Ty.

Quivering with excitement, he nodded.

"Stay here until I'm on the ground, then toss me the bundle. Carefully inch down to the gutter, then jump. I'll be right below."

The night air was chill and damp. It was dark, the moon hidden behind the clouds of the promised storm. Poised precariously at the top of the roof, I felt as though I were looking down into a bottomless pit. Panic knotted my stomach, tightened my throat. Breathing was painful. I'd come this far. I had to go on. There was no going back.

I clung to the thin material of the sheet, my lifeline to the edge of the roof, then to the ground and safety and freedom.

"You all right, Ty?" I asked again.

"Yes."

"I'll go ahead then," I said, still clinging to the makeshift rope, struggling to gain courage. Gradually I slid inch by inch down the splintery shingles, catching the material of my skirt as I did. My heels hit the tin gutter. I winced and gasped. Slowly I exhaled then took several deep breaths.

I turned my body so I lay stretched out, stomach down, suspended. With one hand I grabbed hold of the metal gutter, my other hand still clutching the end of the blanket. I would have to twist my body and grip the gutter with both hands, swing over the edge of the roof, and drop to the ground beneath.

I took another long, shaky breath and closed my eyes. Between clenched teeth I implored God for help. Then I twisted, grabbed, and went over the side. I felt my fingers slip on the slimy gutter, held my breath, and let go.

The fall was harder than I anticipated. I fell on my knees and elbows and toppled sideways onto dew-wet grass.

As soon as I caught my breath, I scrambled to my feet. Cupping my mouth with both hands, I called quietly up to Ty. "I'm down, Ty. It's all right. Come on."

Down tumbled the bundle, nearly hitting me on the head. I put it to one side and squinted up through the darkness, watching the small figure inching his way to the end of the steep roof. The next thing I knew a solid weight of little boy landed in my arms. For a minute I held him close, tears crowding my eyes. "What a wonderful, brave fellow you are!" I whispered over and over as I hugged him.

"Where do we go now, Lyssa?" he asked as I set him on his feet.

His question caught me off guard. It was damp and cold, and the clouds moving across the moon looked dark and frightening.

I'd only managed to think as far as getting out of the inn. We weren't safe yet. Discovery would come with first light, when I was supposed to be up and fetching water from the well, lugging it up to the few occupied guest rooms. Peg would surely sound the alarm if I wasn't on the job.

Then I thought of Francis. He had said he was going to London for a couple days. Surely he was back by now. Of course, *Francis*. No one at the inn knew anything about my friendship with him. It seemed logical we should go first to his cottage. He would be sympathetic, glad we had followed his advice. We could stay there until it was light, then walk to the crossroads.

"I think we should go to Francis Vaughn's cottage. We can wait there until it's light enough to meet the stagecoach."

I picked up our bundle and grabbed Ty's hand. "Come on, Ty. Once we're at Francis's we'll be safe."

It seemed farther to the cottage than I remembered, burdened as we were by our bundle and the darkness. Hurrying along, I hoped I would be able to find the path that turned off the road leading to the village. I realized I was walking too fast for Ty's little legs and forced myself to slow down.

It was slowly getting light when we finally came in sight of the cottage. The relief I felt was, however, short-lived. There was no answer to my repeated knocking. When we both went around and looked in the windows, there seemed to be no one inside. There was no smoke coming from the chimney, nor any sound of movement inside. Ty sat down wearily on the little porch while I wondered what to do next.

Only a little while later we saw a shawled woman approaching. When she saw us, she eyed us suspiciously. To my cheerfully managed "good morning," she just gave me another hard look and a humph. She came right up to the front door without speaking. Her eyes were skeptical.

"We are friends of Mr. Vaughn's."

"Well, he ain't here," she said. "I've come on directions from the owner to clean the place up."

"But Mr. Vaughn—"

She gave me a short grunt and another glance.

"You one of his—" She paused significantly before finishing. "One of them models?" She used the word as if it were something distasteful, wrinkling her nose as she said it.

I drew myself up, feeling offended by her attitude. I knew we looked bedraggled and not at our best; however, I didn't think she had any cause to be so rude.

She got out a key, turned it in the lock, and opened the

door. "There's no use you staying around. He's gone. But left me a job to do, I'll tell you! Paint spots on the rug, rusty, smelly cans he'd used to mix paint and oil! Never saw such a mess. Don't know what he used the kitchen for. Not to cook in, I warrant."

I was ready to ask her if we might come in, perhaps even have a cup of tea, but she was already inside and about to close the door.

"Did Mr. Vaughn leave a message of any kind?"

She shook her head vigorously. "Nor did he leave anything for me, not even a shilling! Just took off, he did. I suspect that's the last we'll see or hear of *him*. Can't see why the gentleman who owns this cottage rented to the likes of him. Humph. An artist." With that she shut the door squarely in our faces.

"Come on, Ty," I said, gathering up our bundle.

He got up a little reluctantly, tired from interrupted sleep, our hazardous escape, and the long walk.

"Where will we go now, Lyssa?" he asked plaintively. "I'm hungry."

"I know, Ty. So am I. But we still have to get away from this village. Once we're on the stage—well, then at the first rest stop, we'll have an enormous breakfast." I tried to sound sure of myself.

"When will that be? Where is the stagecoach?"

For some reason—and all I can credit it to is pure inspiration—the word *sanctuary* came into my mind. I remembered reading that pilgrims, fugitives, and refugees could find a safe place to stay in a church by claiming *sanctuary*. Their captors or pursuers could not violate that.

Not far down the road from Vaughn's cottage I saw the steeple of the gray stone village church rising through the morning mist.

"We'll go to Christ Church, Ty. We can wait safely there until it's time to catch the stagecoach."

We walked the short distance to the church without further conversation.

Cautiously, I pushed the heavy, nail-studded church doors open. At once the combined smell of old wood, cold stone, beeswax, and the faint, decaying scent of wilting flowers prickled my nostrils. This being an Anglican church, I felt sure there would be matins. Soon a sexton would be lighting tapers on the altar, and a handful of faithful parishioners would start coming in for the early service. Surely someone could give us the information we needed.

I tugged Ty's hand and we went inside, almost on tiptoe, as though not to disturb the unearthly quiet. We slipped into one of the back pews. Gray light palely filtered through the high, stained glass windows on either side. I had no idea what time it was. The lack of sleep sent waves of fatigue through my body, which was numbed by the chill and dampness of the early morning.

Ty gave a big yawn and leaned his head against me.

I had to find out from someone when the next stagecoach was due. If I approached the vicar when he appeared, I hoped he would be kind and not ask too many questions. I rehearsed my story nonetheless. He more than likely knew all his regular church members and would recognize that we were strangers. I would just say we were on our way to relatives and had missed our connection. That was literally the truth, though a slightly incomplete version of it.

With a heavy sigh, Ty nestled his head on my lap and curled up on the bench beside me. He was soon sound asleep.

I prayed. This was, after all, a house of prayer. I reached for the prayer book in the narrow wooden niche on the back of the pew in front of me and turned the pages. I came to one called Prayer for Travelers. In the dim light I read the short verse then repeated it silently.

O Lord, our Guide on all our life's journey, protect us from

*all danger as we travel, that accompanied by Thy holy angels
we may arrive safely whither we are going. Amen.*

For the first time in weeks, a sense of tranquility descended like a warm blanket around me. I'm not sure how much time had passed, for I must have drowsed a little myself, when I heard a stirring, the shuffle of footsteps. An acolyte came out to light the candles on the altar. Behind me I heard the church door squeak as it opened and an elderly woman entered. She looked at us and smiled as she passed to take a seat in a front pew.

I eased Ty's head off my lap and slipped the shawl-wrapped bundle under his head for a pillow, then made my way up the aisle to where she sat.

As it turned out she was the vicar's mother, visiting him from the next village, and she had come in on the stagecoach a few days before. She told me that a stage was due in less than an hour. If we waited at the crossroads, it would stop for us.

I thanked her and went back to where Ty slept peacefully. I hated to wake him, but I didn't dare miss the stage. We had come this far without trouble, but I wouldn't feel entirely safe until we were on board the stage and on our way to Briarwood Manor and our relatives.

13

*S*ince it was still early, the stagecoach was occupied by only two other passengers, both nodding sleepily. A few minutes after we boarded, we were settled comfortably, Ty fast asleep.

I was still too tense to relax. I could hardly believe we had made our escape and were finally on our way to our original destination. We had met with so many unexpected delays, endured so many unforeseen hazards, encountered such mean, unsavory characters. The fact that we had survived it all was surely due to God's grace and dear Nanny's prayers.

As soon as we arrived safely at Briarwood Manor, I would write to her and tell her about all our adventures. I had to smile in retrospect, recalling how Nanny appropriated Scripture to fit her purposes—or rather *mine*. "You must be wise as a serpent. The world is a wicked place, and you two are going out there, two lambs where wolves prowl," she had said.

However, considering what had actually happened to us, I realized we had been in more dangerous territory than Nanny could ever have imagined. I had certainly had my eyes opened and was no longer the innocent I had been when I started on this journey.

The unknown threat of Muir still hung over us. I had no idea what he had done or might be doing given Ty's disappearance.

I must have drifted off because the next thing I knew the coach had stopped and I heard the driver bellowing, "Meadowmead! All out for Meadowmead."

"Come, Ty, wake up. We're here!" It is hard to describe the relief I felt. Soon I could turn over the responsibility of my little brother to those older and wiser than I.

We got off the stage in the town square. I was stiff, my muscles cramped and aching from the long trip.

"Just think, Ty, we're almost to Briarwood Manor. You're going to love it there." I picked up our meager belongings wrapped in my shawl.

"How far is it, Lyssa?"

I knew the Hazeltons' estate was quite a distance from the village. I remembered riding to and from the village in my pony cart. However, Ty had already traveled quite a distance, and I didn't want to discourage him at the outset. "Not too far."

Ever willing to accept my word, Ty smiled up at me and we started off. Happy hearts carry a light load, and knowing a warm welcome awaited us at the end of our journey, we were cheerful travelers. We sang some of the songs Nanny had taught us and managed to cover quite a distance before Ty's steps began to lag. His little legs, so much shorter than mine, tired sooner. We stopped by the roadside and rested, then pushed on.

I encouraged Ty by telling him of the delicious lemon sponge cake the Hazeltons' cook made and of the sweet grape juice from their own arbor. Even those promises did not manage to sustain his sore feet, and we sat down under a leafy oak tree.

All I had with me was a crumbling currant bun I'd bought from a vendor the last time the stage had stopped to change horses. I handed it to Ty. Since he was more thirsty than hungry, it did not prove very satisfying.

About this time, we saw a carrier cart coming along. When the driver saw us, he reined his horse and asked us where we were headed. When I told him Briarwood Manor, he offered us a ride.

"Goin' right past it." He nodded. "Come on, get in."

Gratefully I lifted Ty up on the seat beside him, then climbed aboard myself. The driver flicked the reins, and the horse plodded along the rutted country road. The man turned and looked at us. "Is the old lady hiring new help, then?"

At first, I was puzzled by his question. Then I realized how shabby we must have looked. Obviously he thought I was applying for a servant's position at the Manor. When I informed him Lady Hazelton was my mother's aunt, he looked startled.

"And how long is it since you visited your aunt, miss?"

Not willing to tell him my whole sorrowful history, I just said, "Five years."

At this, his bushy eyebrows went up alarmingly. He gave his head a slight shake. "Well, miss, I'm afeared you'll find many changes up at that house."

I felt a sense of uneasiness at these gloomy words, but I hesitated to ask more. In another mile, around another bend or two, we would be there. If there was bad news, I'd learn it soon enough.

The driver didn't offer further comments or questions, and we rode the rest of the way in silence. At length we came in sight of the tall, scrolled iron gates with the arched bridge across the top, the Gothic letters spelling BRIARWOOD MANOR.

The driver brought the wagon to a stop.

"Thank you very much," I said, gathering my things together and preparing to get out.

"You're sure now, miss, this is where you want me to leave you off? It's a long way back to town."

I tried to ignore the uncertainty in the man's voice, but it caused my heart to beat nervously. "Of course," I said briskly as I got down. I helped Ty down. "Thanks again."

He did not reply. Unsmiling, he tipped the beak of his cap, slapped the reins, and drove off.

Resolutely I pushed back the doubt he had triggered in my mind. "Come on, Ty."

I leaned against the gate and pushed it open. It gave a protesting creak, for it was badly rusted.

We went through and started up the driveway. I'd forgotten the house was set so far back from the road. Distances are often distorted in the memories of children.

"How far?" Ty's voice sounded plaintive.

"Not far. Not far at all, now," I answered, knowing it was about a quarter of a mile to the house. "Just think how happy they'll be to see us."

Although determined to be optimistic, the farther we went along the winding drive, the more wary I became. On either side, where I remembered acres of velvety lawn, there was only tangled underbrush and thistles. Weeds seemed to have sprung up everywhere. When we came in sight of the rambling Tudor house, I was shocked to see it standing in the midst of untrimmed hedges that had grown to gigantic height. Shaggy rhododendron bushes drooped with wilted, browning blossoms.

The closer we got to the house the lower my spirits fell. I looked up at windows that had once shone like sparkling jewels from their diamond-shaped panes and saw that they were shuttered. My steps slowed, and a premonition of dread overtook me. Ty began to drag his feet. He was catching my growing sense of dismay.

There was no sign of life anywhere. A kind of stillness hung over the house.

"Isn't anybody home, Lyssa?" Ty's voice was low, a little frightened. "It looks—empty."

It looked worse than that to me. *Haunted* was the word

I'd have chosen. I swallowed hard. "Oh, I'm sure somebody's there, Ty. We'll just go knock on the door. Surely somebody will come. Anyway, we'll see, shall we?" I tried to sound optimistic, something I certainly did not feel.

Ty's little hand tightened in mine as we went up the terrace steps to the front door. I raised my trembling hand to lift the badly tarnished brass knocker. All sorts of dreadful possibilities marched through my mind as we waited for the door to be opened, ones I did not dare pursue. I held my breath, then knocked a second time, somewhat harder.

Had Ty's observation been right? Was the house empty? Had some terrible tragedy taken place without my knowledge? Were my relatives ill or even—I couldn't quite finish that thought.

No communication had taken place between Briarwood Manor and Crossfield Grange for the past five years. My stepfather had curtly cut off my mother's oft-expressed wishes to invite Lord and Lady Hazelton to visit. Even her pleas to have them come for Ty's christening had fallen on deaf ears. My poor mother loved her aunt and uncle dearly and had wept bitterly when they had been banished so cruelly from our lives. I wasn't even sure Muir had notified them of her death.

The Hazeltons were both close to sixty when my mother and I had lived with them before she married Muir. It was possible they had succumbed to the ravages of age in the years since I had seen them. Like their once beautiful house, perhaps they too had deteriorated under the sickle of time.

The longer we stood in front of that closed door, the more frantic I became. If something *had* happened to the Hazeltons, what would I do? Where would I go? How would I care for my little brother?

My heart was literally in my throat. Ty sagged against me. We had come too far, traveled too long under hazardous conditions, to be faced with this. Please, *please,* someone come! I prayed desperately.

As I prayed, my ears pricked up at the sound of slow steps advancing on the other side of the door. The latch slipped back, and the door was inched open.

"Yes, what is it? What do you want?" a quivery voice asked.

I could not see through the narrow crack created by the open door. I bent closer but still could see nothing.

"It is Challys Winthrop, Maria's daughter, and my brother, Tyrone. Are Lord and Lady Hazelton here?"

There was a soft exclamation, like a sigh. Immediately the door swung back, and a small, gray-haired lady stood holding out her arms to me. "Dear little girl!"

It was Aunt Evelyn. I stepped forward into her embrace, my tears of relief mingled with her tears of joy.

"Oh, Auntie Evelyn, I'm so glad to see you. So happy to be here. We've come such a long way—" I almost sobbed. Then drawing away, I reached out for Ty and pulled him forward. "This is Ty, Auntie. We've come to stay. If you'll have us."

"Of course, my darling. Of course!" She hugged me tightly. Then as we drew apart, she looked down at Ty. "And this is Maria's dear little lad. How I've longed to see you."

Aunt Evelyn put her hands on his shoulders, looked down at him. Ty smiled angelically.

"Come in, both of you. There's so much I have to ask."

"There's so much I have to tell you." I was too exhausted and too relieved to be careful. "Mr. Muir hasn't contacted you, has he?"

"Oh, no, my dear. We haven't heard from him in—well, since your sweet mother passed away. We wrote at once to Muir, explaining that we would be unable to come because of George's health, and enclosing a bank note, requesting it be used for a headstone for our dear Maria's grave. But we never heard back from him, and we never learned how the money was spent." She shook her head sadly. "Probably gambled away . . . But we mustn't dwell on those unhappy times. We have to celebrate your coming. Just wait until George hears. Wait until he sees this young man."

Auntie Evelyn beamed, her wrinkled face appearing magically younger, her faded blue eyes sparkling as she regarded us fondly. "Come along, he's in the library."

She beckoned us to follow her down the hallway. "He will be overjoyed to see you. It will do him a world of good to know you have got away from that monstrous man—oh, Challys, George has had much to bear, if you but knew. Now, don't be alarmed. Through all his trials, all his tribulations, George has remained . . ."

She paused, pressed her fingers to her mouth for a few seconds. "Although, you'll find him aged, his spirit is still valiant and . . . Well, come along, dear. See for yourself."

In spite of Aunt Evelyn's euphemistic description, I was shocked to see Lord Hazelton. The tall, erect man I remembered was bent of shoulder, his eyes vague, his face deeply lined. At first, he didn't even seem to know who I was. Aunt Evelyn had to repeat my name several times, saying, "It's Maria's little girl, George, all grown up now. She's come and brought her little brother."

Gradually understanding broke through, his face lit up, and I saw a glimpse of the jovial, energetic gentleman I had known as a child.

I was badly shaken by this visible deterioration in the person on whom I'd planned to unload my burdens, the person of whom I planned to ask advice and direction.

Auntie declared we must celebrate our homecoming, and Uncle George insisted we open one of the few remaining bottles of fine wine still in his once well-stocked cellar.

I tried to enter into Auntie's enthusiasm and hide my shock at the changes that had taken place at Briarwood. The whole house was in a run-down condition due to lack of proper care by a greatly reduced staff. At dinner, I noticed the silverware was tarnished, the elaborate lace tablecloth torn and unmended, the jacket worn by their old butler, Manning, shiny and missing buttons. It was all I could do to put on a good show and help Auntie as she tried to act as though everything was just as it used to be.

Toward the middle of dinner Uncle George became silent, then his head sank to his chest. At a nod from Aunt Evelyn, Manning assisted him out of his chair and led him out of the room. Aunt Evelyn's glance followed his progress anxiously, and she suppressed a deep sigh.

Soon after that I took Ty, who was heavy-lidded and yawning, upstairs to put him to bed. A trundle bed had been placed in the hastily aired room I was to occupy. I tucked him in, and he was soon asleep.

Bone tired and weary as I was, sleep did not come easily for me. The haven I had dreamed of reaching had been an illusion. Here at Briarwood all was ruin and chaos, with as unpredictable a future as my own.

14

The next afternoon, while Uncle George napped, my aunt and I had the opportunity to really talk. We went into her sitting room decorated with flowered wallpaper and lace curtains, a room I remembered as being as feminine and dainty as Aunt Evelyn herself. Now, both seemed a little worn and faded. She told me she had been devastated by the news of Mama's death but had received no word from Muir since. She never received the letter I sent her from school saying I was on my way to Crossfield Grange to get Ty, so she was appalled to get a letter weeks later from Nanny Grace, inquiring if we had arrived at Briarwood.

"After that, I prayed every day for your safety. I worried endlessly about what might have happened. I was terrified that dreadful man had done something with you two. I never trusted him, not from the first moment he came courting Maria. I was proven right."

Auntie shook her head, bit her lower lip. "Nanny warned me not to try to find out anything through him if you had not yet come. She said you had a good head on your shoulders and would take every precaution to cover your tracks so Muir couldn't find you. And that, she suggested, might mean your arrival here would be delayed. That's what I counted on."

I should not have been surprised that my aunt had never received the note Francis Vaughn had promised to post. Given his erratic personality and his self-absorption, I should not have counted on his carrying out my request.

I told Auntie about the stagecoach accident, Ty's illness, and how I was forced to work off our indebtedness to the Brindles. I didn't, however, tell her about posing for Francis Vaughn, nor of my discovery of the stolen goods in the inn's basement. Auntie had about all she could handle at the moment.

"To think you both might have been killed in that accident! And you, poor dear, who had never done a day's work in your life—a scullery maid and tavern worker! At least your dear mother was spared knowing."

From this reaction, I realized it was well I hadn't revealed all I'd endured, witnessed, and been involved in, especially posing for Francis Vaughn. An artist's model was considered on a par with an actress, or worse. Auntie would need more than a whiff of smelling salts if she knew I'd done that.

Although I kept some distressing revelations from my aunt, there was much at Briarwood that could not be concealed from me. After being there less than twenty-four hours, it was clear the Hazeltons had fallen on hard times. The evidence was everywhere—the worn rugs, the upholstery that needed replacing, the shredded lining of faded velvet draperies, the furniture that needed dusting, floors polishing. Of course, what could be expected when the house servants, who used to number twenty, were now reduced to the elderly cook, a laundress that came twice a week from the village, and Manning, almost as doddering as Uncle George.

Gently, I questioned Aunt Evelyn as to how all this had happened. Reluctantly, she confided what had become of the Hazeltons' once vast fortune.

111

During her disastrous marriage to Henry Muir, my mother had turned to them on several occasions to borrow large sums of money, first from the trust fund they had set up for her as her guardians. When that was depleted, they lent out of their own bank account.

"Maria promised to repay us, and I know she meant to. We had no idea what her life was really like with that man. It was only through rumors that we learned of his profligate behavior. Then our bank manager, an old friend of your uncle's, came down from London to talk to us personally. He told us Muir was well known as a gambler, that he frequented notorious gambling houses in the city and was rarely lucky. Thus we assumed some of the large sums we loaned to Maria were to cover Muir's losses."

Although I had been away at boarding school while all this was going on, I wasn't surprised to learn the man I so despised was worse than I had even suspected.

"George was still going up to London to his club in those days," continued Aunt Evelyn. "There he heard Muir was also a heavy drinker. Gradually, we realized the money would never be paid back. Not that we begrudged it, not a cent of it, if it would have helped Maria, whom you know we thought of as a daughter. It was just that, in the end, it made things worse."

The story got even more depressing as Auntie went on. About the same time they had extended Muir credit, Uncle George suffered some severe financial losses of his own. Sugar being highly valuable and its sale here in England quite profitable, Uncle George had invested in several trading ships sent to obtain the prized commodity from the plantations of the Caribbean islands. Several of the vessels were shipwrecked in tropical storms, their entire cargo lost at sea.

"So you see, we became unable to help Maria anymore, and Muir cut us off from her. I suspect he intercepted our letters to her and her letters to us. He wanted to isolate her so he could conduct his derelict lifestyle without any interference."

Tearfully, Aunt Evelyn glanced at me. "I can't tell you how glad I am you are here, Lyssa. I haven't known what to do, and George, dear fellow, well, you see how it is, don't you?"

Auntie looked suddenly old, hopeless. Impulsively, I reached out and covered both her thin, blue-veined hands with my own. Hard as it was for Auntie to tell me all this, I think in a way, it was a comfort to have someone with whom she could share her terrible burden.

It took me only another day at Briarwood to realize Uncle George had only a tenuous hold on reality.

The first night I was at Briarwood, I told them both how important it was to safeguard Ty's future. Uncle George had seemed attentive and lucid. He promised he would discuss it with his lawyers, arrange for me to become Ty's legal guardian, claiming Muir was neglectful and abusive, that he had recklessly squandered what little remained of the estate that was rightfully Ty's through our mother. It was *her* inheritance that had maintained Crossfield Grange. The house and land otherwise would have gone to pay off Muir's gambling debts.

Two days later, when I asked Uncle George if the lawyers were going ahead with the necessary legal procedure, he looked at me blankly. With a sinking heart, I realized he had no memory of our conversation. That's when I realized how dire the situation at Briarwood really was.

That afternoon I went outside into the gardens, or what was left of them, overgrown and choked with weeds as they were, and walked along the gravel paths between the neglected flower beds. I was unable to put my thoughts in any kind of order.

One by one, I counted off the main problems confronting me.

My stepfather's dissolute habits had bankrupted the Hazeltons and destroyed Ty's inheritance. I had hoped to shift *my* problems to responsible relatives. Instead, *their* problems had become *mine*. There was no one else. I would have to take on all I had hoped to relinquish, and more. Uncle George was fast slipping into senility. Auntie was helpless, Ty a mere child.

Everything depended on me.

Because I had no experience in household management, at first I thought the sparse meals served were due to the fact the cook was old, no longer eager to show off her culinary skills. Auntie's explanations seemed feeble. The kitchen garden yielded only a few vegetables because it had been left untended. In the orchards, unharvested fruit fell rotting to the ground. When I offered to do the grocery shopping, having gained some knowledge from my experience at the inn, I found the horses were gone, the three carriages sold. There was no vehicle in which anyone could go to market.

Since I'd volunteered, I took a large wicker basket and walked into town. There I received a further cold dash of reality when the butcher refused to put the roast I selected on Lady Hazelton's account.

"Sorry, no more credit," he retorted, then rudely turned away to wait on another customer, leaving me standing at the counter, red faced and humiliated.

With my empty basket I headed back up the road to Briarwood. Something would have to be done. At once. Or we adults would end up in the poorhouse and Ty in an orphanage or, worse, back with Muir. I had to find a way to earn some money.

What could I do? Ironically, the only kind of work for which I had any qualifications was that of a maid. What good was my fine education at Miss Elderberry's Academy to me now? I could read and speak a little French, play the piano adequately, do five embroidery stitches. I had fine penmanship. Hardly skills that paid well.

I might get a job as a governess. However, that meant living in a home with the children to be tutored. I couldn't leave Ty with Auntie and Uncle, who needed to be taken care of themselves.

Another restless night followed. I woke at heart-pounding intervals, tossing and turning, all the problems and possible solutions tumbling in my troubled mind.

Still distracted the next morning, I tried tidying up the downstairs. The dust and general messiness of rooms once spotless and neat was getting on my nerves. The parlor maid had long ago departed. It was amazing how much clutter collected daily in a house where people, used to servants, never picked up anything or put anything away.

The library was the worst. Uncle never emptied the ashtray where he dumped his tobacco whenever he sat smoking his pipe in the big leather chair. He was, further, in the habit of dropping sections of the newspaper to the floor as he finished reading them. I started gathering them up, then something caught my eye—the classified advertisement section of the *Country Journal*. Picking it up, I sat down and perused the listings under Help Wanted. One seemed to leap right off the page.

SOCIAL SECRETARY TO A LADY. Non-residential position for refined, well-educated gentlewoman, skilled in social protocol, excellent penmanship. Special consideration given to someone who can do calligraphy suitable for dinner party menus, invitations, place cards. Three days a week. Location local. Personal interview after receipt of letter of application. Reply Box 47, this paper.

I read it over twice. Refinement, social grace, good penmanship. It sounded like the requisites taught at Miss Elderberry's. In these, I certainly qualified, and the position was local. The opportunity sounded almost too good to be true, and I had nothing to lose by answering.

A quick search for stationery turned up only a few sheets with the Hazelton crest engraved at the top. It would never do for a letter of application for a secretarial job. I felt it would be inappropriate to associate myself with the Hazeltons. I knew Auntie would recoil at the thought of her niece having to earn money. However, since my last name was different from theirs, I could keep my relationship with them a secret. Pride might be a sin, but it was one of which the gentry of the day were all guilty. I wanted to protect my relatives from malicious gossip.

I decided to walk to the village and purchase some plain, good quality paper. I would say nothing unless, of course, I got the job. Then I would explain to Aunt Evelyn. Crossing bridges as I came to them seemed to have become a way of life for me.

I set off on foot for the village, my thoughts wandering back to my recent escape from the inn. What had been the Brindles' reaction when they had found us gone? Had they discovered the storage room door unlocked? If so, what had they made of *that?*

I shuddered. I wished I could forget that terrible episode in my life. The present was what was important. I turned my mind to the possibilities of being hired as a social secretary, being able to bring some much needed income to Briarwood.

In the stationery store, I looked through the samples of stock, searching for paper that would give a good impression yet was not too expensive. I happened to glance up. Through the front display window of the shop, I saw a tall man crossing the street. Dressed in a caped, tweed coat and fine leather boots, carrying a riding crop in one hand, he was striding directly toward the stationery store. Nicholas Seymour. What in the world was he doing in this remote village such a distance from London?

Immediately, two incidents flashed into my mind—the fog-shrouded morning when he had put Lady Bethune on the stagecoach, and the time he had burst into the inn demanding from Mrs. Brindle an account of his aunt's missing luggage. What would *he* think if he knew what had happened to it? Surely he would have gone straight to the authorities.

All at once I felt guilty. I *knew* about a crime and had not told anyone. Did that make me an accessory? Liable to arrest and imprisonment? A shiver ran up my spine. Instinctively, I stepped back and nearly tipped over a bin of lithograph prints behind me. It tottered precariously and the store owner at the counter glared at me as if I'd done it on purpose. I righted it, then glanced around for a place to hide should Nicholas come into the store. However, I was spared the necessity.

Just as he reached the door, someone hailed him. He turned to greet another gentleman hurrying toward him. Nicholas removed his hat, providing me with a good view of his handsome profile. A brisk wind lifted his thick, dark hair, blowing it back from his well-shaped brow. After a minute or so, the two men broke into hearty laughter and, still talking, strolled back across the street toward the pub and restaurant, The Golden Peacock. As they disappeared inside, I realized I had been holding my breath.

I hurriedly made my choice of stationery, purchased it, and left the store. My avoidance of a man who would hardly recognize me seemed ridiculous. Walking home, I told myself I was being foolish. I'd been able to avoid encountering Nicholas Seymour face-to-face, but it was not as easy for me to stop thinking about him.

That dismal October morning of our first meeting, which now seemed long ago, almost in another lifetime, I'd been too troubled, too preoccupied, to be fully aware of him. However, I had been conscious of a strange current that passed between us. The second time I saw him I'd been too miserable and ashamed to do anything but hide. Yet when Francis Vaughn urged me to imagine saying farewell to a *real* beloved in an attempt to catch the right expression on my face for his painting, it was Nicholas Seymour's face my imagination summoned.

Oh, it was all too absurd. I commanded myself not to be

so silly. To concentrate on the task at hand. To write the letter of application and hope to be hired as a social secretary.

I spent the rest of the afternoon and most of the evening composing my letter, practicing my handwriting, and finally copying the text onto the new stationery in my best penmanship.

The next morning I walked to the village post office and opened a letter box so I could receive mail without giving Briarwood Manor as my return address.

Two days later when I checked the box, I found a letter inside. I examined the address to be sure the letter was for me. The handwriting was a spidery Spencerian, the smooth paper sealed with red wax stamped with a crest. I was astonished to get so prompt a reply, then wondered why we are so often surprised when our prayers are answered.

However, it was the letter's signature that startled me more than its timeliness. It was signed, Isabel, Lady Bethune, Elmhurst Hall, Meadowmead. Nicholas Seymour's aunt! My fellow traveler on the ill-fated stagecoach.

I walked home, conflicting emotions churning within me. A chance for a job had come, just the opportunity I had prayed for. But the identity of my prospective employer was a shock. I had certainly never expected to see Lady Bethune again or to learn that she lived so near Briarwood Manor. The letter said I was to come for a personal interview the following afternoon. Should I go? Would Lady Bethune recognize me? Would she question me about my relatives? Would my need to work reveal their dire circumstances, opening them up to embarrassing village gossip? Instead of helping my aunt and uncle, would I be betraying them? First, I had to tell Aunt Evelyn.

When I went in the house, Aunt Evelyn looked at me curiously. "What is it, Challys? You look very pale, dear. You're not ill, I hope."

I handed her the letter to read. Then, as gently as I could, I explained. She wept a little, saddened that things had come to this. "Not that I blame your dear mother," she quickly assured me. "She was young and foolish and trusting. It's that villain Muir. I blame George and myself as well. We should have seen past his slick facade and kept Maria from making such a terrible mistake. Now, you and dear little Ty are also the victims of our failure."

I comforted her as best I could, and in the end she understood. In fact, she helped me put together a proper outfit to wear for my interview with Lady Bethune.

"You must make a good impression," she said firmly and went to search her armoire for something we could alter to fit me. As so many ladies of her social station, Aunt Evelyn had acquired complete new wardrobes for each season. She still had many hardly worn outfits, although most were two or three seasons out of fashion.

We decided on a blue foulard promenade dress with a fitted jacket and flounced skirt that could easily be lengthened to accommodate the three inches I had on Aunt Evelyn. The material was still beautiful, and when we finished the few nips and tucks necessary for a perfect fit, it looked quite stylish.

We put new ribbons on my bonnet, and Auntie found a pair of kid gloves she had never taken out of the box. A lucky thing, too, because my hands had not recovered from the ravages of my work at the inn. The total effect we created was that of a young lady who may have fallen on hard times, but still had a certain chic and panache.

The following afternoon I walked to the end of the road, waited for the postman's cart, then asked for a ride to the gates of Elmhurst Hall.

Elmhurst Hall was very grand. Built of gray stone, it had turrets and towers and statuary. In the marble-floored foyer, to which I was admitted by a formidable butler, massive portraits of important-looking ancestors lined paneled walls.

The butler showed me into the morning room and told me her ladyship would be with me shortly. The room, filled with sunlight from floor-length French windows that looked out onto terraced gardens, was furnished with gold-leafed antiques, baroque-framed mirrors, and priceless vases containing hothouse flowers—pale pink peonies and amethyst irises.

As I sat there waiting, I tried to guess whether or not Lady Bethune would recognize me from our shared adventure. Probably not. Perhaps the incident itself had become an amusingly told story to relate to friends at dinner parties. It would be far-fetched to think that with her busy social life, the dozens of people she likely met at the rounds of parties she attended, she would remember someone she had met *literally* by accident.

I heard the rustle of taffeta skirts and the staccato tap of heels on the polished floor. The door opened, and Lady Bethune, tall and elegant, swept into the room. Regardless that she was leaning on a gold-topped cane, she carried herself like a queen.

I rose to my feet.

"Good day, Miss Winthrop." She inclined her beautifully coifed silver head. "You are very punctual. I admire that in a person. It shows respect for others' time, a courtesy I find sadly lacking in today's society. Too careless to be prompt, people seem to care nothing for keeping others cooling their heels."

She sat down in a needlepointed chair with gracefully curved arms and pointed to its twin with a ring-encrusted hand. "Do sit down."

When I did so, she said, "Now tell me about yourself."

Briefly I recounted my education at Miss Elderberry's.

"Yes, yes." She made a dismissive gesture. "Your letter told me all that. What I'd like to know is why a pretty, young girl like yourself would want, or *need*, such a job? It will be rather dull, shut up here three days a week with a cantankerous old lady, writing thank you notes of various kinds, accepting invitations and turning them down."

She regarded me with a curious and penetrating gaze. "I have the strangest feeling I know you. I usually have no memory for names, though I never forget a face; yet, somehow your signature struck a chord. Challys Winthrop." She paused. "Is it possible? *Have* we met?"

I saw no reason to lie and no way to avoid the truth.

"Yes, my lady, we have met. Last October we were both passengers on the same stagecoach. Unfortunately, there was—"

"*Of course!* Why in the world didn't I place you at once? Now it's all coming back. You had a child with you, did you not? A little boy?"

"Yes, my brother."

"I recall he was very spunky about the whole deplorable affair. You were calm and resourceful. Not like *most* silly young girls would be. That ninny Thompson, my maid, never did get over the fright. She left me, can you imagine? Once we got home. Her nerves were shattered, she said. Stuff and nonsense. She felt some guilt that our belongings were never recovered, as though it were her fault, that I somehow blamed her."

At once, the picture of Lady Bethune's ruined alligator tea case in the Brindles' storage room flashed into my mind, and I suffered a pang of guilt at the knowledge. But Lady Bethune was rattling on, and I tried to focus my attention on her.

"Well, good-bye and good riddance, I say. I cannot abide people who let unforeseen circumstances overwhelm them." She pursed her lips. "Now it's all coming back. You did not go on with us the next day, did you? Something happened . . ." She broke off frowning as if annoyed at her faulty recall.

"Ty, my brother, suffered a bad chill. He became ill and was too sick to be moved. We had to stay and—"

That's as far as I got with my story because suddenly we heard men's voices from out in the hall.

"Is my aunt at home?" came a deep authoritative voice.

I felt myself tense. A moment later the morning room door opened, and there in the arched doorway stood Nicholas Seymour.

"Nicholas, dear boy! Come in!" Lady Bethune exclaimed delightedly. "The most marvelous coincidence has just occurred." She gestured toward me. "This young lady came in answer to my ad, and it turns out she and I had a previous meeting."

His gaze fell on me and lingered there. I felt warmth rise into my cheeks, and I experienced the same erratic heartbeat I'd felt at our first meeting. I'm not sure how long we stared at each other. Only a few seconds perhaps, surely no longer. I felt the planet spin under my feet, and somehow I knew nothing would ever be the same for me again.

Thank goodness, as Lady Bethune began explaining to Nicholas in detail the amazing coincidence, I had a few moments to regain my composure. During her recital, Nicholas walked into the room and stood by his aunt's chair, outwardly attentive to her, but looking at me. When she finished her tale, she asked, "Isn't that the most remarkable thing you've ever heard?"

He smiled slightly, his expression unreadable. "You mean the *very same stagecoach* that had the accident, the one I tried to talk you out of taking?"

"Oh, fiddle, Nicholas! Do you always have to prove yourself right?" Lady Bethune said impatiently. "But, yes, the very same. And as you can see, I'm paying for not taking your advice with this foot!"

She turned to me, touched her foot with the tip of her cane. "I twisted my ankle badly when we were struggling out of the overturned carriage that night. I didn't notice it too much at the time. It's given me a great deal of trouble ever since. That's one reason I need someone to help me do things."

"You mean fetch and carry for you, don't you, Aunt Isabel? I hope you don't plan to hire Miss Winthrop to take the unfortunate Thompson's place?"

"Of course not!" Lady Bethune said indignantly. "If she takes the position, which I'm certainly going to offer her, she'll be answering invitations, paying my bills, writing cheques, that sort of thing. She has very fine handwriting."

Again I felt his amused gaze on me, and again I blushed.

123

"Pay no attention to Nicholas, Miss Winthrop, he's a terrible tease." Lady Bethune gave him a severe look. "Sit down somewhere, Nicholas, and let Miss Winthrop and me get on with our business."

To me she said, "Just ignore him."

If that were only possible! I tried to follow her suggestion, but I could not forget his presence in the room, nor his gaze on me.

Lady Bethune made quick work of the rest of the interview and offered me the position at a wage far higher than I had expected. Stunned, I agreed.

"Good. Well, then, can you start right away, next week?"

"Yes, that will be fine." I got to my feet, pulling on my gloves, ready to depart.

Nicholas immediately rose and sauntered toward me. "I gather you live locally, Miss Winthrop?"

I hesitated, uncertain as to whether I should give my address as Briarwood Manor and reveal my connection with the Hazeltons.

"Yes, just a little past the village."

"Then I can give you a ride. I'm going in that direction."

I glanced at Lady Bethune, who had not been quick enough to conceal her surprise. Noting it, I asked him, "But haven't you just come to visit your aunt?"

Nicholas exchanged an enigmatic look with Lady Bethune, who took her cue and said, "Haven't you forgotten this is my afternoon to play whist, Nicholas? My friends are coming at three, and I must take my nap beforehand. Perhaps you can attend to whatever business you have in the village and join me for dinner this evening."

"Splendid idea, Aunt Isabel. I *did* forget. So, you see, Miss Winthrop, I will be killing two birds with the proverbial stone by giving you a ride into Meadowmead and transacting my business too."

I had planned, after my interview, to wait at the end of the road for the postman's return trip or the carrier cart going to the village. Since I did not want to divulge my true identity to Nicholas Seymour, I decided I would ask him to leave me off at the town square.

Accepting a ride with him meant I would have to walk back to Briarwood Manor in Auntie Evelyn's too small, French-heeled boots. A small price to pay, I decided, for the chance to ride beside Nicholas Seymour in his shiny, gold-trimmed phaeton pulled by a fine black horse.

In the weeks that followed my coming to work for Lady Bethune, I employed diverse ways of keeping my relationship with the Hazeltons a secret. With some self-reproach, I realized I had become quite adept at being covert. For a person who had hitherto prided herself on honesty, I was collecting quite a number of secrets and half-truths. I'd conspired with Nanny to take Ty away from his father. I'd concealed from the Brindles the true state of my financial situation when Ty became ill. I'd told neither Lady Bethune nor Nicholas Seymour about the stolen goods stored at the inn. The only person I'd confided that to was Francis Vaughn, who had advised me to keep quiet about it. Francis was also the only one who knew about my brief career as an artist's model, and no one knew about *him*.

For my short years I had racked up quite a series of less than honorable positions and activities.

At the end of each day's work, I walked out Elmhurst Hall's drive and concealed myself behind the high boxwood hedge at the gates. The road was one used by carriers, workmen, and farmers on their way to and from Meadowmead, and someone always gave me a ride home.

This became more and more difficult, however, as Nicholas began appearing at his aunt's house nearly every day I was there. He always had a viable reason—he happened to be a weekend guest at some friend's country place or had come down from London on some estate business or had just dropped by to see how his aunt was faring.

He would slip into the room where his aunt was dictating

replies to me or I was working at the desk. It was quite unnerving. The minute he appeared I became acutely aware of his presence, though I tried to keep my attention on my work while he remained idly chatting with Lady Bethune about mutual friends or regaling her with the society gossip she loved to hear. If I attempted to leave quietly, he would be on his feet at once, purportedly with errands to do in the village, and offer to drive me home.

The game of keeping my background a secret became harder and harder to play.

As the Scottish poet Robert Burns so aptly wrote, "The best laid plans of mice and men often go astray." So did my intention of keeping my relationship with Lord and Lady Hazelton to myself.

With my first month's salary from Lady Bethune, I took Ty to town to buy him some badly needed clothes. He had outgrown the hand-me-downs the inn's cook had passed on to him, and he was badly in need of new boots.

We were just coming out of the village shoe store when we almost collided with Nicholas.

"Upon my word! What a happy coincidence!" A broad smile lighted his usually rather stern expression. "Miss Winthrop! And who is this fine little fellow?" he asked looking down at Ty.

"My brother, Tyrone," I stammered, taken completely off guard.

Ty, of course, had not been with me at our first meeting, that day I was on my way to kidnap him, and the day Nicholas had come to the inn, Ty had been nowhere in sight. Nor had I subsequently mentioned Ty.

"Ah, then this is the plucky lad my aunt told me about. From what I heard about you, young man, you were as brave a fellow as anyone could want in a disaster. My aunt was very impressed."

Nicholas then looked at me, raising his eyebrows. "I think

this calls for some kind of reward. On behalf of my aunt, I'd like to buy this fellow a treat. What do you say to that?"

I felt Ty tug my hand. His upturned face looked hopeful.

"That is very kind of you, Mr. Seymour, but not necessary."

"I never do things because they're *necessary*, Miss Winthrop, only when it pleases me to do them. Come along, then, shall we?"

16

We were soon seated at a corner table in the nearby cozy tea room and surrounded by delicious smells of roasting coffee, cinnamon, and chocolate. While Ty made a serious study of the pyramid of goodies on the tray the waitress presented for his selection, Nicholas addressed me.

"I really owe *you* a debt of gratitude, Miss Winthrop. My aunt's disposition has taken a decided turn for the better since your coming to Elmhurst Hall. I had been getting quite concerned about her. The injury she sustained in the accident was more serious than she led you to believe. It has confined her severely, limiting most of the activities she enjoys.

"It was unlike her to become morose and depressed, but at her age, I think she felt most of the joy of life was over. There has been a remarkable change in her now that she has a cheerful, young companion three days a week, even though I think she may be hard put finding enough for you to do each time. It is important that she has something to look forward to, and I am very grateful to you for offering your services."

Overwhelmed with such extravagant praise, it seemed less

than honest to allow him to think my answering the ad was the sort of thing an idle young lady with time on her hands might do for a lark. The time to lay my cards on the table, so to speak, had come.

"Mr. Seymour, I would not have you laboring under a false impression of me. I did not offer my services to Lady Bethune out of sympathy. In fact, I did not know of her injury until the day I came to apply for the position."

I paused, meeting his direct gaze. "While *you* may never do anything out of necessity, others are not so fortunate. I *needed* employment and had few qualifications other than the ones outlined in your aunt's advertisement."

I glanced at Ty. "I must earn my living and support my little brother."

"I understand," Nicholas replied. "I find you refreshingly honest, Miss Winthrop. It is a quality I hold in high regard. I would be disappointed if you were anything less."

Ty tapped my arm and in a loud whisper, asked, "Could I have the strawberry pie with cream *and* an apple tart?"

I was about to say, no, choose *one,* when Nicholas responded instead.

"Of course, you may have whatever you want." He smiled over Ty's head at me, chiding teasingly, "A growing boy, Miss Winthrop!"

After we'd finished our tea, there was no way I could refuse Nicholas's offer to drive us home. I was glad I had taken the chance to explain our true situation. Otherwise, Nicholas might have been startled when he drove up to Briarwood Manor. He would have had to be blind not to see the condition of the grounds, the forsaken look of the house itself.

As we came to a stop in front and Ty scrambled down, I turned to Nicholas. "My aunt and uncle are not receiving just now. My uncle is elderly and not well. I hope you understand why I cannot invite you in."

He held up one hand. "No apology, please, Miss Winthrop."

However, at that very moment, Aunt Evelyn, alerted by

the unusual sound of carriage wheels on the gravel drive when she had long since stopped entertaining or welcoming guests, came out onto the stone steps. At the sight of the splendid phaeton and my handsome escort, she looked abashed. I saw her hands flutter to her hair, then smooth down her skirt.

It was then, I believe, I came to admire Nicholas Seymour in a new way. He treated Auntie with elaborate courtesy, making the most gentle and tactful conversation with her. If aware of her discomfiture at her present circumstances, he seemed to consider them of no account and strove to put her at ease. I recognized then the gentleness and consideration under his urbane, confident facade, which might even be taken for arrogance.

Before he departed, he asked Aunt Evelyn if he might call on us next time he was down from London. She assured him he would be most welcome. When he turned to me, as if for confirmation, there was a look in his eyes that left me quite breathless.

I was glad the truth was out. In the days that followed, I felt more relaxed and able to enjoy going to Elmhurst Hall. Lady Bethune treated me kindly, the work was easy, and the surroundings were luxuriously pleasant.

The longer I lived at Briarwood Manor and worked for Lady Bethune, the further away the whole awful experience at the inn seemed. It got so that entire days passed when I didn't even think about it. But when I did, I felt cold shivers run up my spine. Sometimes I woke up at night terrified by dreams in which I was caught and accused of being the Brindles' accomplice. These dreams became less and less frequent, however, and I intentionally tried to put the memory of those dreadful times out of my mind.

I still worried about Muir tracing us, though. I wondered if my absence from Miss Elderberry's had been reported to him. Had he investigated my whereabouts or put Ty's disappearance together with that of my own? Or did he even care? Having depleted my mother's fortune, perhaps he had nothing to gain by finding us. Perhaps he remained in a drunken stupor unable to think or act.

On the days Uncle George seemed more alert, I approached him about consulting his lawyers about adopting Ty. He always agreed, but nothing was ever done. In two years I would be twenty-one, legally of age. Then I could adopt my brother myself. In the meantime, I lived from day to day, hoping for the best.

Almost a week to the day he had met Aunt Evelyn, Nicholas called on us. He arrived with a bouquet of flowers for Auntie, a box of fine cigars for Uncle George, a box of assorted French chocolates for me, and a large red ball for Ty. He conversed on many subjects, tactfully ignoring Uncle's vagueness. He revealed a fine mind as well as a sense of humor.

After he left, Auntie declared him charming. She told me she had often heard people speak highly of him. "However, he's thought to be a confirmed bachelor," she said with a slight twinkle in her eyes. "Many a debutante's mama has hoped to net him for her daughter. He's avoided capture—until now."

After that, whenever he was down from London, which was more and more often, Nicholas called at Briarwood Manor. On the days I worked for Lady Bethune, he drove me home from Elmhurst. These were always happy occasions. Nicholas was an interesting, well read, and amusing raconteur. His humor was never cruel; he had a tolerant way of looking at other people's foibles and laughing at his own.

Auntie's remarks about Nicholas's eligibility and his invulnerability to marriage-minded mamas made me curious. Even though I couldn't deny my attraction to Nicholas, I tried not to allow myself any fantasies about him. After all, he was a sophisticated, worldly gentleman, widely traveled, well educated, and at least ten years older than I. For all Auntie's insinuating comments, I doubted Nicholas had romantic feelings for me. Gratitude for my lifting his favorite aunt out of the doldrums was probably closer to the truth.

At Elmhurst Hall, the household staff became used to my presence, as did Lady Bethune's frequent visitors, so much so I often worked at the desk in her sitting room while she entertained guests. When her three special friends came to have tea and play whist with her, I was often amused and sometimes scandalized by the society gossip they exchanged.

One afternoon while addressing invitations to a party Lady Bethune was planning to give at Elmhurst when the gardens would be in full bloom and she would be rid of her cane, I overheard fragments of the ladies' animated discussion. In spite of myself I was drawn to listen.

"Indiscreet isn't the word for it!"

"Blatant, I'd say!"

"If they had only used some—"

"Discretion?"

"No one would have been the wiser."

"But Neville Cuthcart! Never!"

"Typical male."

"There's blame enough all around."

"She's always been headstrong."

"Wild as a March hare. I've known her all her life."

"Well, she's done it now."

"Lost everything, I heard."

"Not quite."

"What do you mean?"

"She managed to slip her portrait out and sold it."

"*Sold* it, to whom?"

"A commercial company that is using it—"

"*Using* it? How?"

"On candy boxes, playing cards, powder tins, and soap wrappers."

Loud gasps all around.

"*No!*"

"Surely not?"

"Indeed. She got scads of money for it and—"

"You don't mean it."

"I do, and she's off to France."

"*France!* But the scandal of it—"

"In France it will be considered fashionable."

A spatter of laughter followed this remark, then I heard Lady Bethune's voice cut through the levity.

"That may be all well and good now, in France, as you say. But in *England* even the *whisper* of scandal is social death. No matter how long she stays abroad, she'll never be received here by anyone again."

A murmur of agreement went around the table.

Though I felt a small, undefined sensation at Lady Bethune's pronouncement, that bit of gossip about an unknown lady of quality who had lost her social standing soon faded from my mind.

I finished my work that day and slipped out, leaving the ladies still playing cards. I found Nicholas waiting outside in his phaeton.

"What are you doing here?" I asked, genuinely surprised. "I thought you were in London."

"Spur of the moment decision." His eyes were full of mischief. He helped me into the buggy, and we started off down the drive. "However, if you believe *that,* you must also believe in providence? Do you?"

"Do I what?"

"Believe in providence? Some call it fate, chance, or coincidence. Think back. Don't you believe it's a remarkable coincidence we have crossed each other's paths before and now you are my aunt's social secretary and the two of us have become friends and are driving along this country road in this particular part of England?"

I had to laugh. "Well, when you put it that way—"

"Aha! I'll tell you that even on that first morning, when I put Aunt Isabel on that stagecoach and saw you, I *knew* we were bound to meet again."

"Do you have such premonitions often?"

"No, not at all. That's what makes that one so remarkable."

I started to tell him about the second time our paths had crossed so strangely, that day at the inn when I was a scruffy maid, my arms full of laundry, and he, a fine gentleman, came striding in, demanding information from Mrs. Brindle. In fact, I was tempted to tell him the whole of my experience at the inn, but we were turning into the gate of Briarwood Manor, and as we came up to the front of the house, Ty came bounding down the steps to greet us. Later I fervently wished I had told Nicholas then about my experiences at the Brindles', but the opportunity was lost.

Nicholas, who had become quite a hero to my little brother, got out and spoke to Ty fondly, tousling his curly head. "Want to give Seneca a lump of sugar?" he asked.

He took a small rock of sugar out of his pocket, placed it in Ty's hand, lifted him up, and told him to open his palm and hold it out to the horse.

Seneca gobbled it up, and Ty shrieked happily. "It tickled!" he shouted. We all laughed.

After inviting us to go on a picnic with him down at the river the next afternoon, Nicholas said good-bye and rode off.

"I like him, don't you, Lyssa?" Ty asked me as we went hand in hand up the steps and into the house. I didn't have a chance to answer because Aunt Evelyn was waiting for us, holding a letter she had received that day from Nanny Grace.

The letter was in reply to the one I had sent to her at her sister's, telling of our safe arrival at Briarwood Manor. I read it eagerly, but its contents alarmed me and revived some of my old dread. Nanny wrote she'd heard from Lily, Mama's former maid who had left to get married.

When Muir sobered up and found us gone, he had gone into a wild rage, cursing and threatening everyone. He had summoned the sheriff to Crossfield Grange, ordered him to issue a warrant for my arrest and to send out men to track me down.

The local constabulary had reason to dislike Muir because of his frequent brawls in town taverns, his violence, and his brutal dealings with tenants on the farm. The sheriff had been heard to say that any child would be better off without a father like Muir, so it was possible the man had not followed Muir's directions regarding the matter.

Lily also reported that Muir was constantly drunk, shut up in the isolated house. He had sold most of the furniture, paintings, and silver, dismissed all the servants who had not left in disgust. The villagers assumed he would eventually drink himself to death.

Nanny concluded by saying she prayed every day we would remain happy and safe. I put aside Nanny's letter, echoing her heartfelt prayer.

It seemed to me that more than enough time had passed. If we'd not yet heard from Muir, maybe the villagers were right, maybe he'd already drunk himself to death. Was it safe to feel safe? I wondered. Perhaps it would all work out for us. Apprehension soon gave way to anticipation, however, for the next day Ty and I were to go on a picnic with Nicholas.

Nicholas's idea of a picnic, I discovered, was far different from the haphazard bun and apple sort on which Ty and I had gone during our time at the inn. Even the April day itself, full of sunshine and soft breezes, could not have been more perfect if Nicholas had ordered it himself.

Nicholas took us to a lovely spot on the parklike grounds of Elmhurst Hall, where swans glided gracefully on a placid pond, and from where, every now and then, a doe and fawn could be seen in the nearby grove of aspens.

With a great flourish he spread a linen cloth on the ground, brought out silver and plates, then lifted a large wicker hamper from his buggy. He dispensed its contents, an array of delicacies that would have delighted the most particular gourmet. Our feast consisted of rolls of thinly sliced ham stuffed with chicken salad, pâté spread on wedge-shaped wheat wafers, hothouse pears and chilled grapes, assorted

French pastries, lemonade served in crystal glasses, and hot tea sipped from porcelain cups.

Nicholas was a wonderful storyteller and kept Ty raptly listening to tales of derring-do. He also had a repertoire of limericks and jokes that made me laugh until tears came and had Ty rolling on the grass with irrepressible laughter. Nicholas, at play, was not the stern, rather arrogant person I had believed him to be at our first encounter. In fact, I could not have imagined a more delightful companion.

After we'd eaten, Nicholas produced a cribbage board and taught me to play while Ty sailed a toy boat at the edge of the water.

It was a day of simple relaxation and fun, and when it came to an end, I felt sorry. I realized it was the first such day I could remember having since I was a child. It was the first of many such happy days spent with Nicholas, more often than not with Ty, as well, who was forming a real affection for Nicholas. I appreciated Nicholas's interest in my brother, who had been sadly in need of a strong male figure in his life.

I had been Lady Bethune's secretary for over two months when one day Aunt Evelyn called me into her sitting room.

"We must have a serious talk, Challys. Sit down, my dear." She patted a place beside her on the cushioned window seat. The sun streaming in through the diamond panes behind her created a halo of light around my aunt's gray hair, giving her a slightly angelic aura. The expression on her face, however, sent a rush of alarm through me. She took my hand in both of hers and began.

"You have been here long enough to observe and understand the situation in which your uncle and I find ourselves. I'm sure I don't have to elaborate." She shook her head. "However, I have always been one to face things squarely and not indulge in self-pity. Things are as they are, and we must make the best of whatever circumstances in which providence sees fit to place us.

"I need to discuss Tyrone's future, and yours, Challys, as

they are irrevocably linked. What *you* do inevitably affects him. That's why we must plan your debut carefully."

"My *debut,* Auntie?" I wondered if my aunt had lost her senses. A debut in our dire financial condition? Debuts for young ladies involved a fortune in various expenses. Surely she couldn't mean a fancy ball to introduce me to society.

"Yes, of course. It is the only possible way for you to meet an eligible man to marry, one of prestige and wealth, the kind you *must* marry to insure Ty will have a proper education at Harrow or Eton and then at Cambridge or Oxford."

Auntie halted for a moment at what must have been my shocked expression, then went on. "All this takes a great deal of money, Challys. It would be different if George and I were able to provide you with a large dowry, as once we might have done. Now that is out of the question, so I've taken matters into my own hands."

I could think of nothing to say to all this, so I just waited for Auntie to proceed.

"Fortunately, we still have connections in society. I have given George's health as the reason we no longer go out or entertain. However, I have a dear friend, Lady Prudence Cahill—we were schoolgirls together and have remained in touch through the years—who is willing, in fact happy, to be your sponsor, to launch you into society by giving you a ball at the end of the summer and, if you make a good impression on her, of which I have no doubt you will, perhaps even a London season."

I stared at Auntie, protest ready, but I didn't have a chance to speak.

"No, don't interrupt, dear. Let me finish. We have corresponded, and she is enthusiastic about the plan. She has married off several granddaughters very successfully to men of rank and wealth. She loved doing it and is eager to do it again. She is coming to meet you and discuss her ideas with you as to the theme of the ball, the invitations, and all the details."

Auntie looked so pleased with herself I didn't have the heart to tell her how I felt about such an arrangement.

It was only later in my bedroom that I gave way to my true feelings. Ty, who now felt at home at Briarwood, had been moved to the small room next to the old nursery. I was glad for the privacy, as I was overcome with emotion. The fact that my debut was a *fait accompli,* arranged without my knowledge or consent, stunned me. For nearly seven months I had been on my own, making my own decisions, caring for my brother, working under the most trying conditions. It had given me strength and independence. I had lost touch with how things were done in the world of society, which Aunt Evelyn still inhabited, the one into which I'd been born as well.

An arranged marriage, based on the man's property and position, was the accepted custom in society. A girl of good family had only to be personable, socially graceful, and pliable. This had remained unchanged. It was I who had changed. A marriage based on achieving security was repugnant to me, but what Aunt Evelyn had pointed out was true—Ty's future depended on my entering into the proper marriage. But a loveless one?

Restlessness made sleep impossible for me that night. Everything Auntie said had sounded reasonable, even justifiable. Yet something within me recoiled. I didn't want to be traded for financial compensation. Somewhere in my girlish dreams, deep in my romantic heart, still dwelled the hope of one day knowing a forever love, a mutually spontaneous one, the kind I'd read about in novels and poetry. Was this hope to be denied me for my brother's future?

Without willing it, Nicholas Seymour came into my thoughts. For the first time, I allowed my true feelings about him to surface. I recalled how my pulse leapt when he walked into the room, how I relived our most casual conversations. I saw his face, those keen, gray eyes full of intelligence and humor, the mouth I had once thought so stern, smiling, its expression transformed. His gentleness with Ty especially touched me. I saw him lift my little brother up into the saddle and to Ty's delight lead him around the circular driveway several times. Nicholas Seymour may have entered my life by accident, but he had invaded my dreams, captured my heart. If only *he*...

Quickly I banished that possibility. It was wishful thinking and futile. By all accounts, Nicholas had had many opportunities to marry and yet remained a bachelor. I told myself it would be silly to think his interest in me was anything but platonic.

That night I wept foolish tears, relinquished my dreams. Marrying the *right* man to ensure Ty a good education, his rightful place in the world, was my duty. I could not refuse the means to accomplish that. Whatever they were. A debut ball was the accepted stepping-stone. I convinced myself I must take the opportunity Auntie and her friend offered.

When morning came I had resigned myself to my fate. At breakfast Auntie told me Lady Cahill would be coming for tea the following afternoon.

Shortly after my meeting with Lady Cahill, plans for my debut into society at a summer ball held at her country estate were initiated.

The weeks leading up to my debut ball were hectic. There had to be many fittings for the extravagantly beautiful dress Lady Cahill's dressmaker was making for me. Even though I tried my best, for Auntie's sake, to appear happy and grateful for all she and her friend were doing, a shadow hovered over what should have been a lighthearted time of gaiety and anticipation.

Until a week before the ball, I continued going to Elmhurst Hall three days a week. Lady Bethune was interested in hearing all the details of my debut. She wanted to know every person on the guest list and had comments to make on each one. Strangely enough, my final week at Lady Bethune's, Nicholas never appeared.

All summer he had come down from London each Friday and most often spent the weekend, visiting his aunt and calling on us at Briarwood Manor. It took every shred of willpower not to ask Lady Bethune about his absence. Fortunately, she volunteered the information. Nicholas had sent word that certain matters kept him in the city. I felt inordinately disappointed.

Then on my last day of work, Nicholas appeared.

In my sudden confusion, I blurted out the question I'd been determined *not* to ask—had he received an invitation to my ball and, more importantly, was he coming?

His smile was enigmatic as he replied, "Of course, I wouldn't miss it."

Afterward, I could have bitten my tongue. I wished I'd not given him the satisfaction of knowing it mattered to me at all whether or not he came. Of course, it *did*.

It mattered most dreadfully.

What hurt the most was that it did not seem to occur to him that my debut would change everything for me. For *us!* Even if our relationship was only a friendship, it had meant a great deal. However, if my ball accomplished what Auntie and Lady Cahill hoped it would and I attracted some eligible wealthy man and became engaged, well, then I could not spend time with Nicholas, even on the most casual basis.

How much I would miss that.

17

As the day of the ball neared, I tried to hide my increasing depression as I went through all the expected and necessary preparations. The night of the ball, Auntie fluttered around me as I dressed. *She* was thrilled and delighted.

My gown was a gorgeous creation, a divine shade of azure blue satin with an overskirt of Valenciennes lace. A Grecian bertha edged the neckline, setting off Mama's matching sapphire and diamond pendant and earrings. I was thankful I'd held on to them.

In spite of it all, I felt heavyhearted as Auntie and I left Briarwood in the carriage Lady Cahill had sent for us. I kept telling myself Ty's future was at stake. I must be witty, charming, and flirtatious.

Ironically, we had to pass Elmhurst Hall on the way to the Cahill's estate. For a moment I wondered if Nicholas would come to the ball as he'd promised, or if the bouquet he had sent was a substitute for his presence. The enclosed card contained a mysterious message, written in his bold, slanted handwriting: If you know the language of flowers, you will understand the meaning.

Nicholas loved riddles and conundrums. He was always trying them out on Ty and me. What was he saying with these flowers?

A debutante traditionally received many bouquets on the night of her debut. Among all I had received, I'd chosen his to carry, a single perfect white rose surrounded by mignonette.

Ignorant of the language of flowers to which he'd referred, I asked Auntie to explain the symbolic meaning of his bouquet.

"He praises your youthful beauty, offers you admiration and affection."

I was touched by the tenderness of his message, yet in my heart of hearts I wanted more than admiration and affection from Nicholas—I wanted deep passionate love, hopeless as my desire was.

When we reached the Cahills', for Auntie's sake I put on a bright face, my most radiant smile. Light shone out from the long windows, and as we mounted the steps into the house, I heard music playing.

We were greeted by Lady Cahill and her stout, jovial husband and led into the ballroom, aglitter with myriad candles in crystal chandeliers reflected in mirrors on the walls.

Almost at once I was surrounded by potential dance partners. One by one, Lady Cahill introduced me to young men, all of whom asked to write their names on my dance card. Lady Cahill looked so pleased, I assumed they were all on her list of eligible suitors.

Whirled onto the polished floor, I was soon caught up in a sense of excitement any girl would enjoy. I danced with one charming partner after another in a dizzying assortment of schottisches and waltzes.

At one short pause between sets, to my surprise, Nicholas appeared. In a black swallow-tailed jacket, white satin waistcoat, batwing collar and silk cravat, he looked more handsome than ever. With his usual assurance, he bowed slightly, then offered his arm to lead me out for the grand promenade.

As I looked up into his eyes, I saw something different in them and felt a ridiculous surge of happiness, a fantastic hope that something wonderful was about to happen.

When the promenade ended, Nicholas took my dance card and crossed out every other name, substituting his own. Until midnight, we danced every dance together. I was dizzy with delight, floating on a cloud.

When the other guests went into the dining room to partake of the sumptuous buffet supper, Nicholas took me into the conservatory, which adjoined the ballroom.

The abundance of ferns and tropical plants and the heavy perfumes of the exotic flowers Lord Cahill cultivated created an Eden-like atmosphere. The murmur of voices and music faded into the distance, and we were alone. We could have been on some enchanted island, the feeling of intimacy was so complete. Nicholas took both my hands, twirled me around in front of him, his gaze sweeping over me.

"In case I did not tell you, Challys, you look beautiful tonight. But, then, you have always seemed so to me." He smiled, then said more seriously, "I had not meant to speak so soon. I meant to let you have your moment in the sun, let you enjoy the experience of having these eager chaps buzzing about you like bees around the loveliest of flowers.

"However, I find myself gripped by the basest of emotions—jealousy. I cannot bear watching. I'm afraid someone else will somehow attract you, and I shall miss my chance."

Still holding my hands he drew me closer. His voice lowered and his eyes seemed to deepen in color as he searched my face. "I discovered I am unwilling to risk losing you to someone else, so I decided to throw caution to the winds and not wait any longer to tell you."

"Tell me what, Nicholas?" I asked breathlessly.

"*What?* Haven't you guessed? That I love you."

"Love me?"

"Yes. Of course. Madly, truly, completely. Couldn't you tell? I love everything about you—your sweetness, your strength, your sincerity, your loyalty, the sound of your laughter, *everything*. I adore you."

Then Nicholas drew me even closer and after an eternal moment, kissed me. It was a tender kiss that slowly deepened. It had in it the promise of passion that even my inexperience recognized and responded to; it was a kiss that forever made impossible my ever belonging to any other man.

When at last it ended, Nicholas held me at arm's length. "Now, do you believe what I said about our meeting being more than mere chance?"

I looked at him with wonder. "Yes, I do believe it, Nicholas." I felt my eyes mist with tears.

Immediately Nicholas whipped out an immaculate white handkerchief and dabbed my cheeks. "No tears. Not ever. If I have anything to do with it, there will never be any more tears for you." His smile was tender. "Oh, my darling, I am going to make you so happy there will never be a need for tears."

Suddenly I felt a marvelous warmth, as though a silken blanket had been thrown about me, protecting me from all the hardships and danger of the past, securing me from any possible harm in the future.

That night, which was supposed to be my introduction into society, was successful in a way no one could have predicted. Even though everyone, including Lady Prudence Cahill, declared delight at Nicholas's proposal, they all seemed shocked—the confirmed bachelor whisking out of circulation the newest debutante of the season. It was unheard of. Everyone was stunned. Nicholas wanted our engagement announced immediately, the wedding planned for three months hence. "Impossible!" Aunt Evelyn, Lady Bethune, and Lady Cahill protested in unison.

"December, then," conceded Nicholas reluctantly. "That is all the longer I am willing to wait," he declared adamantly.

Auntie Evelyn, and even the imperturbable Lady Bethune, were amazed, to say nothing of the circle of society that had written off Nicholas as impervious to the wiles of hopeful young ladies and their mamas.

I felt a passing sympathy for Lady Cahill, who had gone to so much trouble and expense to launch me. However, she dismissed my apologies, saying she had never married off one of her protégées so quickly, nor to someone of Nicholas's caliber. She assured me she was as happy as I was.

But she couldn't really be *that* happy. My happiness knew no bounds.

Now I could express all my pent-up longings and secret feelings for Nicholas that I had kept buried, thinking they were impossible. I could hardly believe I had won the love of such a man. I basked in his loving, protective attitude toward Ty and me. He was everything I could have asked for. He was generous and had a sense of humor, as well as having the qualities I most admired—integrity, intelligence, and kindness. For the first time since childhood, I felt completely loved, cared for, and protected.

A few weeks later we were strolling through the garden at Lady Bethune's when Nicholas presented me with an engagement ring. It was not the traditional diamond or birthstone gem often given as an engagement ring, but one especially crafted from Nicholas's own design. It was a gold, sculptured lily with a large, rosy pearl nestled in the center and tiny diamonds scattered on the opening petals like dew drops.

"Oh, Nicholas, it's beautiful," I murmured as he slipped it on my finger. "It's the loveliest ring I've ever seen."

"I wanted you to have something unique, a ring unlike anyone else's, a symbol of our love."

Our promise to each other was sealed that day with the ring and a kiss. I felt Nicholas's love enfold me like the petals of the lily, and I felt myself opening up to that love like a bud to the warmth of the sun.

Two things endeared Nicholas to me even more and made me realize further how fortunate I was. First was his determination to start legal proceedings to adopt Ty. Second, when I confided to him my reluctance to leave my aging relatives in their failing health and impoverished state, he promptly told me he had been considering offering to buy their estate, renovate the house to its former splendor, and make it *our* home.

I moved through those weeks before our scheduled wedding in a haze of happiness, not knowing just how fragile happiness can be.

18

Ours was to be a winter wedding, set for the first week in December. By then the renovations at Briarwood Manor would be finished, providing a perfect place for the reception following the ceremony. Auntie was in seventh heaven, consulting with decorators and drapers, picking out fabrics for curtains and new upholstery. Uncle George seemed to regain some of his old buoyancy with all the activity around him. Ty, who worshiped Nicholas, was wild with happiness that Nicholas was to become his brother and legal guardian. It all seemed too perfect.

Alas, it was.

Early in November I went to Lady Cahill's London town house, where she gave a reception to introduce me to some of her friends and Nicholas's London friends whom I had not yet met. It was a lavish affair and duly described in the society pages. Lady Cahill tried to persuade me to stay on with her and have some of my trousseau gowns made by the exclusive dress salon she herself patronized. Nicholas urged me to do so and thus what was to have been a weekend visit lengthened into a two-week stay.

Returning late one afternoon, I found an envelope addressed to me propped against the mirror of the dressing table in the guest room I was occupying. Curious, I picked it up, examining the London postmark and the special delivery notation at the bottom left-hand corner. The handwriting was lavishly decorative. Perhaps it was a congratulatory note from one of Nicholas's London friends whom I had not met.

I tore it open, and the moment I saw the signature, I felt my knees weaken. Francis Vaughn! I'd never in the world expected to hear from him again. In fact, I'd purposely tried to forget my experience with him along with that terrible time at the Brindles' inn. It was as if that whole episode had happened in another lifetime, to someone else. But at the sight of his name, it all came rushing back.

I sat down on the bed, took a deep breath, and began reading the letter.

My dear Lyssa,

When I recently read in the society news of the engagement of a Miss Challys Winthrop, niece of Lord and Lady Hazelton of Briarwood Manor, to the Honorable Nicholas Seymour, my first thought was how quickly fortunes can change! Yours for the better, and sadly, mine for the worse. Life is certainly full of odd turns and twists, peaks and valleys, is it not?

Reading of the marvelous shift in your future, I could not help but remember the thin, little barmaid with frightened eyes and a look of desperation whom I befriended little more than a year ago at the country inn. There was something appealing about your face that attracted my artist's eye, but more, I was moved to compassion by your plight. I'm sure you haven't forgotten how, out of the kindness of my heart, I offered you a way out of your misery.

Fate provided for both of us at that time. You were the model I was seeking for a special painting I had been commissioned to produce, and the fee I paid you for posing gave you the money you needed to escape from the den of iniquity in which you were trapped. And trapped you were. You knew of the criminal activities going on there and yet did not report them to the authorities for fear of being arrested as an accomplice. I remember how afraid you were when you told me of your knowledge of this. I suspect you never did report the Brindles. In that case, you are still in danger of being charged as an accessory to their crimes.

Fate has chosen to have our paths cross again. I hope, again, to our mutual benefit.

Much to my crushing disappointment, the painting for which you so willingly posed was not my key to fame after all. When I returned to London to present the finished painting to the man who had commissioned it, I found he had gone abroad, leaving no word as to the date of his return.

I had spent the last of the advance he had paid me on a magnificent frame befitting the subject matter and found myself financially depleted. I found myself without funds and without a place to stay.

In London, I could not afford a suitable studio or apartment. I have been reduced to living and working in a rat hole in one of the worst sections of London. I have written my sponsor numerous times, telling him that the painting is ready and I need to be compensated for this fine work of art, but so far there has been no response. Needless to say, I have reached a state of near despair.

So why should all this concern you? To put it simply, reciprocity. Did we not become friends at a time when you desperately needed a friend? Do not friends have concern and sympathy for one another, the willingness to aid each other in times of trouble?

Because I banked everything on the successful acceptance of the painting for which you posed, thinking it would provide a way into my sponsor's circle of wealthy friends, people who would admire the painting and offer other commissions, the failure of this man to live up to our agreement dealt me a devastating blow. I have been deeply depressed and unable to paint. My debts are piling up daily, and time is running out for me. I was at the point of self-destruction when fate stepped in once more.

Inspiration struck as my eyes fell again on the beautiful completed painting of you as the lady of the castle bidding farewell to her beloved knight. With a few deft strokes of my brush, I could make certain changes that would enable my selling it to a commercial enterprise! I could alter the medieval costume into a diaphanous Grecian-style robe and present the painting to a company that could use it to sell cosmetics. This has been done successfully before. Quite spectacularly so, as a matter of fact, although it was quite a scandal at the time. The portrait in question was of a well-known, albeit notorious, lady of society. It made her a financial fortune, which she needed badly at the time.

When this thought occurred to me, a second one followed. It would be unseemly to have the image of the bride of such a prestigious gentleman as Nicholas Seymour appear on soap wrappers, talcum tins, hairpin boxes, and cologne bottles used by shop girls, perhaps even by women of infamous character. Yet it would certainly save the day for me.

I am reluctant to confront you with this possibility, Lyssa, because you were such a nice little thing, and I grew quite fond of you during the time we spent together. I am sincerely glad you have found a wealthy protector, who possibly is ignorant of your past. However, as you once said yourself, desperate times require desperate actions, and I am desperate.

I am sure Nicholas Seymour would be shocked to see an image of his beloved fiancée, garbed as a woodland nymph, displayed throughout Britain, purchased for a few pennies.

To put it bluntly, I need money, enough so I can travel to France, and pursue my career without financial worry. I'm sure as the future Mrs. Nicholas Seymour you can secure 1,000 pounds, an amount that will eliminate the necessity of my selling the altered painting commercially.

If you ignore this letter and my request, I may be forced to go to Mr. Seymour himself, tell all, and secure from him sufficient reimbursement for my painting of you and for my silence concerning the things in which you were involved at the Brindles' inn. As they say, a word to the wise and all that. I feel sure you will agree the sooner this is arranged the better. I will give you until next Monday to deliver the money. Better you come in person with the money. I don't trust the post, or the people in this miserable slum where I'm now forced to stay. Come to the pub, Dauntless Dan's. I'm there every day at four. It is a neighborhood tavern where I go for my one daily meal and pint. The address is at the bottom of the letter. I will expect your response by return post at the same address.

Yours more in regret than retribution,
Francis Vaughn

My heart pounded. My fingertips tingled. A deep shudder left me weak. The letter slowly slipped from my hands. Within the minutes it had taken me to read the letter, I was transported back to those Sunday afternoons when I had posed for Francis Vaughn at his studio in the woods. I remembered all that he had told me about himself as he painted. So much of it had gone in one ear and out the other, preoccupied as I was by my own problems. Now fragments of those dark confidences came into my mind—his sad childhood, the tragedy of his father's experience in debtors' prison, his obsessive fear he might fail and suffer the same fate, his strange moods. I remembered that sometimes when depressed, he drank heavily, and I recalled how he confessed to taking chloral.

All this came flooding back to me as I sat on the bed shivering at the thought of what Francis threatened.

I leaned down and picked up the pages of the letter, looked at them again. The paper was filled with ink blots, many crossed out words and underlinings. It looked as if it had been written by someone in a chaotic state of mind, perhaps a mind under the influence of drink or drugs. He had told me that after some of those periods of induced oblivion, he could barely remember what he had done. He had added that such times were perhaps better forgotten.

Was this one of those times? Having posted this letter, would Vaughn have forgotten he had written it? Another shudder shook me. No, that would be too easy. This was real. His threat was real. A man I had thought merely an erratic artist had become a dangerous enemy.

I don't know how long I sat there, paralyzed by the contents of his letter. I knew the price of scandal. If something as sordid as this came out, it would mean the end of everything. How could a man of Nicholas's position marry someone rumored to be an artist's model, worse still, an accomplice of thieves? At the thought of losing Nicholas, I felt sick and trembly. Not only would I lose the man I loved, but with him would go my brother's future, my relatives' hope of a comfortable old age.

Something else came into my mind—the conversation I'd overheard among Lady Bethune and her friends, the story of the lady who had sold her portrait commercially and fled to escape the swirl of scandal. I didn't remember all the details. What I *did* remember was Lady Bethune's unequivocal statement: "In England even a whisper of scandal is social death. She will never be received by anyone here again."

I shuddered, remembering the tone of her voice. Nicholas was her nephew. Whatever scandal touched him would spill over onto his relatives. I thought of Lady Prudence Cahill, who had so graciously sponsored me, staking her own reputation by doing so.

I got to my feet and began pacing back and forth. I *should* have told Nicholas *everything*.

I had, of course, told Nicholas about my having to work as a maid to pay off my debt to the Brindles. After I recounted the daily humiliations, the heartless treatment I'd received, to say nothing of the physical toil, he had taken both my hands, turned them over, and kissed the palms and fingertips.

"My poor darling," he'd said, "how courageous you were! All that is now in the past, and we never need speak of it again. I plan to fill your life with so much happiness that those awful times will be forgotten."

Oh, if that could only be true! If only I could forget.

Nicholas had listened with such tender sympathy then; surely if I'd told him the rest, he would have understood how desperate I'd been. Now it was too late to expect either understanding or sympathy.

I put both hands to my throbbing temples.

If this horrible letter had accomplished one thing, it had proven that there were some things from which even Nicholas's love could not protect me. This unexpected threat had the power to ruin all my bright dreams.

Although my afternoons at Francis Vaughn's studio had been perfectly innocent, they could be made to sound shameful and incriminating. The other threat seemed almost worse—my knowledge about the stolen goods, among which were Lady Bethune's belongings. How could Nicholas ever trust me, knowing I'd withheld that information?

The more I thought about it, the worse my situation seemed.

There was no way out but to meet Francis Vaughn's outrageous demand. But how? Where could I get the kind of money he wanted? And in less than a week. All I owned of any value were the few pieces of sapphire and diamond jewelry my mother had left me. I had no idea what they were worth. Family heirlooms were not meant to be sold. Even if I knew where to sell them, I was sure I would not get what they were worth. They had belonged to my father's family, the Winthrops, before he gave them to Mama as a wedding gift. They were priceless, in one way, yet would they pay my ransom?

That's how I saw my situation. I was a hostage, a prisoner to Vaughn's sick mind, his desperate greed. There was no way out. There was no one in whom I could confide, no one to advise or help me. I would have to agree to Vaughn's terms. Maybe then I would be free.

Pleading a headache, I didn't go down to dinner that evening. Lady Cahill was going out to the theater and then to a supper party. She had a tray of soup and tea sent up to me and stopped in to check on me before she left, telling me she hoped I'd be better in the morning.

Of course, I wasn't. I was worse.

I had hardly slept at all. I had spent most of the night staring into the darkness, feeling the darkness was really an abyss opened up before me by Vaughn's threat.

I felt sick at having to give in to Vaughn but felt I had no alternative. Worse than my fear of the possible scandal that would blacken not only my name but that of my brother, my dear aunt and uncle, and Nicholas, was my anguish at keeping the whole situation from Nicholas. But, I asked myself, wouldn't it be worse if Vaughn carried out his ugly threat? I must at least try.

As painful as it was, I decided I must find some way to sell Mama's jewels. If it was for less than the amount Vaughn had asked for, I'd have to get the rest some other way.

I had to take advantage of my being in London. Surely in a big city I could find a discreet jeweler to whom I could sell my heirloom set, without becoming the focus of gossip. I didn't know how I would explain the missing set if anyone should ask. Likely, only Aunt Evelyn would notice they were gone. I would have to make up some story . . .

A chill went through me. I recalled something I'd learned in childhood. "Oh, what a tangled web we weave when first we practice to deceive." I was finding out just how true that saying was.

That afternoon I had to manufacture an excuse for my errand. "Another fitting?" Lady Cahill's eyebrows lifted. "I've never known Madame Sophie not to get measurements right at a single session. Perhaps she is getting on in years though."

Feeling guilty for maligning the poor seamstress to fit my purpose, I left the house, my jewels secreted in their velvet pouch in my muff.

The need for lies multiplied after my first foray into the city looking for a place to sell my jewelry proved unsuccessful. "In for a penny, in for a pound," Nanny used to say. Quoting my dear nurse made my face burn with shame. What would she say about this situation?

I remember little about the next few days. I moved in a trance, motivated by desperation, frantic with fear.

After another day spent vacillating in front of two fine jewelry stores, I lost heart and nerve. On the very threshold of one, I turned away. I could not bear parting with the only possessions I had from my beloved mother. My reluctance overcame desperation.

I dreaded the questioning looks any reputable jeweler would give me for wanting to dispose of such exquisite pieces of jewelry. What I needed was someone who would not ask embarrassing questions, someone who dealt with people in desperate circumstances. I needed a pawnbroker. A pawnbroker would give me cash and would hold my jewelry for a certain length of time without reselling it. Perhaps, somehow, I could find a way to buy it back myself.

Coming back into the house, I noticed Lord Cahill's study door was open. He and Lady Cahill had gone to a dinner party, and the evening paper he was reading before they left was on his desk. It struck me that I might find the name of a pawnbroker in the classified section. I darted in, folded the paper under my arm, and returned to my room. There I scanned the pages, searching desperately for the information I needed. I was amazed there were so many.

One particular advertisement caught my eye.

LADIES AND GENTLEMEN IN TEMPORARY FINANCIAL DISTRESS will find prompt aid without embarrassment. Courteous, confidential. Contact William P. Mossberger.

An address followed. I tore it out, put it in my purse, determined to contact Mr. Mossberger.

At dawn, I wrote a letter to Vaughn stating that I intended to meet his deadline but that I needed more time to collect the amount he had specified. I asked for two more days past the deadline. I signed only my initials. Using the address of the pub, I addressed the envelope, then slipped out of the house before anyone else was awake, scurried like a frightened mouse to the corner, and slipped the envelope inside the postbox.

Luckily, Lady Cahill, busy with her own social life, assumed I was happily occupied with various errands pertaining to my trousseau. She accepted all my explanations of visits to milliners, glovemakers, and shoe shops as plausible. She even excused my distracted air as that of a bride-to-be, her wedding only three weeks away.

I was very much aware of how little time I had to accomplish what must be done. With each passing day, the danger that Vaughn would grow impatient and contact Nicholas increased.

19

*G*iving one of my now well-practiced excuses, I went out, caught a hansom cab at the corner away from the house, and gave the driver Mossberger's address.

When the carriage came to a stop and the driver hollered down to me, "Here you are, miss," I was shocked. This part of the city was a strong contrast to the streets of exclusive shops where I'd been shopping for my trousseau.

Timidly, I walked up to the door of the shop, identified as that of a pawnbroker by the three brass balls hanging over the entrance. The window was dusty, dead flies clustered in its corners. At the edges of a display of clocks, watches, musical instruments, and an assortment of jewelry were a heartbreaking number of wedding rings.

I hesitated. Would this kind of appraiser really know the value of my heirloom set? Well, I was here now. I might as well find out. If the price didn't seem right, I wouldn't have to proceed.

The day outside was overcast, and when I stepped inside I felt like I was entering a cavern. The interior of the shop was dingy, musty smelling. Slatted blinds on the tall rectangular windows at the back allowed little light to sneak in, leaving an overall gloom. Filled with self-disgust at my errand, the urge to turn around and leave was strong. Anger rose up in me at Vaughn's betrayal, which had brought me to this place. But there was no turning back.

The floor was bare and uneven, and my footsteps echoed hollowly as I walked toward the counter. There, visible behind a wire cage, I saw a bald man who looked up at my approach. "Yes, miss, what can I do for you?" His voice was oily and his eyes disappeared into slits as he squinted at me.

I stepped closer, swallowed, then said in a whispery voice, "I would like to have you appraise some jewelry."

"Well, let's see it."

Trying to conquer my distaste, I brought out the velvet bag, opened the drawstrings, and laid the beautiful sapphire and diamond earrings and pendant on the wooden surface. I watched his bony hands with their dirty nails reach for the set and draw it in. He fitted a cylindrical viewer to one eye and bent over to examine them.

The price the man quoted shocked me back to reality. "You must be joking! They are worth far more than that."

He shrugged. "Take it or leave it, miss." His mouth twisted in more of a smirk than a smile.

Indignantly, I scooped up the set, replaced it in the velvet bag, turned on my heel, and walked out, letting the door with its tinkly bell slam shut after me.

For about two hours I walked those grimy streets and went in at least three more such shops. Each time I had to gather my courage, swallow my pride. Each time the price offered was lower than the first had been. Finally, it was getting late, the day darkening quickly. Maybe I should have taken Mossberger's offer. Half-blinded by angry tears, I marched back down the street and into his shop.

To my sorrow, I received a harsh lesson in the ways of the world. The shrewd pawnbroker, guessing what had happened, what had brought me back, lowered the amount of his first offer.

I didn't trust myself to speak. I mumbled something about thinking it over and dashed out. I almost ran to the corner, where I hailed a passing cab. Inside I hunched in the corner, stared out at the dismal early evening. A day lost, I thought, a day closer to the danger of giving Vaughn reason to act. By the time I got back to Lady Cahill's I had a screaming headache.

Upon my return I found a bouquet of hothouse roses had been delivered from Nicholas. In it was a note saying he was sorry to have missed me. He was on his way down to the country. There he would stay with Lady Bethune while meeting with the architect who was overseeing the renovation and remodeling at Briarwood Manor. One wing was being built into a private apartment for us after we were married. Nicholas had spent a great deal of time in the country, busy with all the details of the construction.

I placed the beautiful roses in a vase and set it on my dressing table. Nicholas had been so generous to us all, so kind, so thoughtful. Bitter tears sprang into my eyes. I did not deserve Nicholas's trust and love.

I was to go home to Briarwood that weekend. I'd been gone two weeks and was anxious to see Ty and my aunt and uncle. Nicholas would still be at Elmhurst. I was both longing and dreading to see him. Nearly numb, I returned to Briarwood, uncertain about Vaughn and what he would do, but most uncertain about my future.

Auntie thought I looked tired, and she was right. "You probably overdid in London," she chided gently. "Do try to get proper rest. You don't want to be a pale bride on your wedding day."

My wedding day! Would that ever be?

Nicholas would be riding over from Elmhurst that evening, so I had to bathe and change. As I sat at my dressing table, brushing my hair, I became more and more nervous. The thought of what I was withholding from him made me so weak and dizzy I had to put my head down on my knees to keep from fainting. When I raised it, I saw myself in the mirror. My eyes looked shadowed. Nicholas had always complimented me on my clear, candid eyes. They were no longer so. "Liar!" I accused my reflection.

Later, when I went downstairs, I looked into the drawing room. Nicholas had arrived and was sitting on the floor with Ty, helping him build an enormous edifice of some kind with the marvelous set of blocks he had given him. Suddenly, a similar scene flashed into my mind—Ty playing with the old wooden Noah's ark Francis had found for him at that dark little cottage in the woods. The memory was so vivid, I swayed slightly and reached for the door frame to steady myself.

At that moment, Nicholas looked up and saw me. His smile was quickly replaced by a frown. "Lyssa, darling, what's the matter? You look as if you've seen a ghost." His tone was teasing, but he looked concerned.

For a moment, I could neither move nor speak.

Nicholas's frown deepened. "What's wrong?"

Auntie, too, glanced at me from where she sat working on her needlepoint. "What is it, dear?"

Quickly, I gathered myself together, forced a smile, and brushed aside their questions. "No, no. I'm fine. What a splendid building you two are constructing," I said, turning everyone's attention to Ty's project.

"Indeed," Nicholas agreed, laughingly. "In a few years I predict your brother may become another Christopher Wren."

Later that evening, when Auntie had taken Ty up to bed, Nicholas said seriously, "I think I'll encourage Ty to choose architecture for a career. He has the talent, an innate sense of proportion. He's such a—"

Nicholas stopped, looked at me quizzically. "You're not

listening, are you? There *is* something wrong. What is it, darling? You've seemed distracted all evening."

"Have I? I'm sorry. I guess there's so much to do right now, so much to plan . . ."

"I don't want you worrying and overdoing. I never wanted all this fuss of a big wedding. It was both our aunts' idea mostly, and I assumed, like most young ladies, that *you* had dreamed of one. I assure you, I'd be every bit as happy to have a small, private ceremony, just call everything off."

His words, meant to comfort me, chilled me. *Call everything off.* Maybe that's what we should do. Maybe, that's what *would* happen. Unless Vaughn was paid. Unless . . .

"Oh, of course not, Nicholas. Auntie would be terribly disappointed. She's enjoying every minute of all this. I am just tired. Shopping and so on."

He accepted my denial, but left earlier than usual, saying I should get a good night's rest.

On Monday, I went back up to London on the pretext of more fittings. In reality, I was determined to delay no longer, to swallow my pride, to pawn Mama's jewels.

The following morning I woke up in Lady Cahill's guest room to the sound of pelting rain. A sheet of gray veiled the windows, and a gusty wind bent bare-branched trees in the fenced square below. A morning to match my own depressed mood.

When I came down to breakfast dressed to go out, Lady Cahill exclaimed, "Surely you're not going out on a day like this?"

"Yes, I must," I replied, trying to get a sip of tea down my fear-constricted throat. I could not tell her that tomorrow was my new deadline to come through with the money. I couldn't put it off. I had to go to that dreadful pawnbroker, take what I could get for Mama's jewels, meet Vaughn at his pub, and beg his mercy for the amount I was short.

From Lady Cahill's expression, I'm sure she would have continued questioning the necessity of my going if it had not been for a minor domestic crisis in the kitchen with her new cook. After a whispered conference with the butler, she hurried out to settle it, leaving me free to leave without further explanation.

I knew Lady Cahill would offer me her carriage, but I couldn't allow that, knowing my destination. Outside I put up my umbrella and hurried to the end of the street. Passing all the impressive houses, I thought how shocked their residents would be if they knew my errand. At the end of the street, on the main thoroughfare, I hoped to hail a passing cab.

There were no cabs in sight. The drivers were probably busier than normal, due to the weather. With my umbrella tugged by the brisk wind, my skirts dampened by the driving rain, I walked several blocks in the shivering cold. I finally sighted a hansom and waved for it to stop. I gave the driver the address of Mossberger's pawnshop and settled back, feeling miserable and sick. I tried to convince myself I would not have to leave Mama's jewels in the keeping of that shifty-eyed pawnbroker for too long.

Somehow I would find the means to redeem them before they were resold. Maybe I should take Auntie into my confidence. Perhaps among all the valuables at Briarwood Manor there would be something of less sentimental value we could sell to buy back the sapphire and diamond set.

If only I'd had the courage to tell Nicholas the whole story.

As we bounced along the rain-slick cobblestone streets, another thought struck me. Maybe I should meet with Vaughn before taking the last step of pawning the jewels. If I met him face-to-face, reminded him of our friendship, the desperate situation I was in, and how much harm his threat promised to do to me, to Ty as well, maybe I could convince him to relent. It was worth trying, wasn't it?

Impulsively, I knocked on the ceiling of the cab. When the driver opened his little box and poked his head through, I raised my voice above the drumming of the rain and told him I'd changed my mind. I gave him the name of the tavern Vaughn frequented. Surely there was an enclosed side for ladies. There I could wait until Vaughn showed up.

"That's down on the waterfront, miss. You *shure* that's where ya wants to go?" The cabbie's voice was doubtful.

"Yes. Dauntless Dan's," I repeated, willing my voice not to shake.

"If you say so, miss." The cabbie still sounded uncertain, but he closed the box and we went on. I peered out the rain-spattered window. The streets we were now passing were meaner, more squalid. Dim figures huddled in doorways, shabby women, ragged children with old faces, drunks. I shrank back, frightened. I'd never been in this part of London nor seen such poverty, such degradation. No wonder the cabbie had seemed uncertain.

Then with a sudden jolt, the cab stopped. The driver opened the ceiling flap again. "This is the closest I can get, miss. There's sumpin a going on up front. A right crowd there is. You *shure* this is where you wanted to go?"

I sat forward. "What do you suppose is the trouble?"

"Can't say, miss. People runnin', jamming the way. Don't rightly know. There's always sumpin goin' on down in this part of town. I don't want to get messed up wi' it, I can tell you that. I'm goin' turn around, miss. You goin' get out or not?"

I pushed open the window, leaned my head out to see for myself. Clusters of people moved in groups, spilling out from the sidewalks onto the street directly ahead of us, ignoring the shouts of wagon and cab drivers. I caught sight of a helmeted policeman trying to stem the flow of the crowd.

Whatever was going on, I still had to meet Vaughn. I couldn't wait. "Will you wait for me?" I called up to the driver. "I've promised to meet someone. If he isn't there, if I can't find him, I'll come back."

The driver began shaking his head, but I rushed on. "It won't take long to just check. I'll pay extra. Please wait."

I got out, gingerly holding my skirt high. The street and

sidewalks were filthy. Above the huddled backs in the crowd, I saw the weathered sign of Dauntless Dan's swinging in the wind-driven rain. I moved cautiously forward. The stench was terrible—unwashed bodies, rotting garbage from overflowing trash cans, the rank smell from the river just beyond. As I inched toward the tavern, I heard comments from the people crowded around the entrance, their thick cockney accents almost unintelligible to me. I strained to hear what was happening, what excitement had created this crowd. What I heard shocked me.

"Poor sod."

"'Ad it comin' to 'im, I'd sy."

"Reglar braggart him."

"Alus talkin' big. Jest t'other night he was buying drinks for the house, tellin' everone within earshot 'e'd come into some big money. Reglar windfall, 'e called it."

A murmur of anticipation and excited whispers rippled through the crowd. Someone close to me said, "They're bringin' the body up from the river now."

The crowd surged forward, creating a passage for me to slip through. It closed behind me almost immediately, and I was wedged tightly at the very edge of the pushing crowd.

"What's happened?" I asked breathlessly.

A shawled woman next to me shoved her wrinkled face right into mine. I could smell whiskey and onions. Opening a toothless mouth, she said, "They found some poor bloke a bobbin' in the water and dragged 'im out. Seems his throat's been cut."

I gasped, instinctively drawing back in horror, but I found I couldn't move. People were crowding ever closer, hoping to catch a glimpse of the action. There was nothing I could do but stand there horrified as a stretcher, carried by two hefty men, passed not two feet away from me.

A gray canvas sheet had been thrown over the body, but one arm had slipped off and dangled stiffly off the side closest to me. My eyes locked on that hand. Nausea overcame me. I clenched my teeth, trying to control it. With all my strength, I twisted around, elbowed and pushed my way through the thick wall of people until I managed to emerge on the other side, gasping hungrily for air.

I stumbled forward just as the strident clanging of a bell shrieked through the foggy air. A police ambulance clattered down the street. I looked around frantically for my cab, praying the driver hadn't left. Spotting him among other stalled vehicles at the next corner, I picked up my skirt and ran.

I was shaking violently as I yanked open the door, pulled myself inside, and closed the door shut behind me. Panting, I fell back against the shabby leather seat.

The driver looked down at me through his box. "Nasty bit, that wuz, eh? Now where to, miss?"

For a minute I was too shaken to reply. Where to, indeed. What now? I leaned my head back and closed my eyes. Weakly, I gave the driver Lady Cahill's address, and we started again. It was all such a nightmare. I hadn't seen Vaughn, nor had I taken the jewels to be pawned. Nothing had been accomplished. Another day had passed, bringing threatened disaster nearer.

I don't remember much about that long ride from the waterfront, with its grim streets and grinding poverty, to the elegant, treed, fenced square with stately Georgian houses. I felt drained of all feeling, except horror.

Lady Cahill was standing in the front hall, speaking with her maid, when I came in the front door. Her expression underwent a quick change when she saw me.

"My dear child! Whatever has happened? You look ghastly. Are you faint?" She came toward me, her taffeta train rustling behind her. Her hand on my head felt refreshingly cool. I closed my eyes, wishing I could erase the scene I'd just witnessed.

"Dora, take Miss Winthrop up to her room immediately. Help her out of these wet clothes. I'm afraid you're coming down with a chill," she said to me. "I told you you shouldn't go out in this frightful weather. I'll send up some hot water at once."

Within minutes I was upstairs, Lady Cahill fussing over me. I was wrapped in warm blankets, my feet soaked in steaming water, my damp hair dried. I was tucked into bed with a flannel-wrapped heated brick at my feet, quilts piled on top of me.

"Now, there you'll stay, young lady. Nicholas would be very cross with us if you came down with something so close to the wedding. I'll send up a hot toddy to take away the chill."

If only it were that easy to take away the deep chill within me. I shuddered. Nothing could reach that.

The hot toddy made me drowsy, and I slept fitfully off and on that afternoon. Later, waking from dreams haunted by the scene at the waterfront, the unresolved threat still hovered. I had to find a way to contact Vaughn, to keep him from going to Nicholas. But making another trip down to Dauntless Dan's was too much to contemplate.

As I lay there in the darkened room, slowly the graphic picture of the murdered man on the stretcher passed through my mind's eye. As if I were standing there at the edge of the crowd again, I saw the gray, bloated hand swinging from the stretcher.

A scream caught in my throat. I sat bolt upright in bed, clutching the covers to my chin. I knew that hand! I recognized it! Many times I'd seen it holding a brush, raised in a flamboyant gesture, covered with paint. On the little finger was the onyx signet ring he wore. The man they'd dragged from the river was Francis Vaughn!

Every nerve in my body quivered and twitched as over and over I saw the image of the shrouded figure on the swaying stretcher. I huddled under the blankets, unable to stop shivering. Strangely, the realization that his death meant I was free from his threat was slow in coming. Neither did I feel immediate relief. Who could rejoice over such a savage death? Who could have murdered him? Was it premeditated, or had Francis simply been in the wrong place at the wrong time? Even mistakenly killed?

I shuddered. I knew I couldn't be mistaken. The ring I could not forget. Unless someone had stolen it from him. Unless robbery had been the motive for his murder. But

Francis, by his own admission, was without means. Why would anyone think differently? Was he the victim of a random assault?

Endless questions pounded in my mind. I had to find out. Surely a brutal murder like this would be in the newspapers. I would have to get hold of a paper, though that would take some doing. Ladies were not supposed to read newspapers. Ladies were considered too delicate to be exposed to the harsh facts of life printed in their pages. Fathers or husbands usually removed the society and household sections for them.

Just then Lady Cahill peeked in to check on me. "Feeling better, my dear? Nicholas sent word he is coming up to London tomorrow afternoon."

I assured her I would be fine by then, and she went away, leaving me to my own dark thoughts.

Nicholas! I had hardly thought of him for hours. I had been too distraught over my experience at the waterfront. Now, however, I realized that Nicholas might never have to know *anything!* The threat was gone. Yet, something lurked in my heart and peace eluded me.

The next morning, when Dora brought up a breakfast tray, I risked asking her if she would fetch me the morning paper, if Lord Cahill had left his.

She gave me a surprised look, then said in a low voice, "Oh, miss, there's been the most horrible murder! I seen the headlines when I placed the paper on his lordship's desk. It's enuf to give you the creeps, miss."

Dora didn't seem to think it odd I wanted to read the account. She soon returned with the paper tucked under her apron and produced it with a conspiratorial flourish.

I didn't have to search for the article. It was right there on the front page.

POLICE FIND BODY OF MURDER VICTIM
A body found floating in the river near the waterfront early yesterday, and first thought to be that of a drowning victim,

was in fact that of a murder victim. Examination revealed death was caused by a knife wound to the throat. Police assume the victim was then thrown into the water. Although there was no identification found on the body, persons at the scene identified the man as a regular patron of Dauntless Dan's, a local tavern. Witnesses testified the victim had been drinking heavily the night before, buying drinks for other customers, and flashing a large sum of money. Further questioning of these same witnesses indicated the man was a sign painter who called himself an artist. He was known to have taken jobs in exchange for meals and drinks. It was discovered he rented a flat, which he used as a studio, under the name Francis Vaughn. Police are asking for information as to next of kin or any other help in locating persons who may know the victim or any motive for his killing.

It *was* Francis Vaughn. But how could I go to the police? I had no information other than the ring I recognized. I had no idea where Francis came from, who his family might be, or even if he had any relatives.

For the rest of the morning, I fluctuated between elation and despair. To be free of the shadow of scandal that had hung so heavily over me the last week was wonderful. But at what cost? A man's murder? There was still the question of the painting. What had Vaughn done with it? Where was it? Had the police found it among his belongings when they went to his flat? Had he already altered it? Was it possible the painting would surface at some later date?

As I changed and dressed for Nicholas's visit, I debated whether I should tell him everything. I had been through so much since I last saw him. I had held our future precariously at the brink of a disaster that could have destroyed everything for us, including his reputation, our families' honor, my brother's welfare. Miraculously, it had not happened.

Although I had not been forced to lie to Nicholas, I'd withheld the truth. Could I go into a marriage with someone I loved and respected carrying the weight of such a dark secret?

The thing I was most ashamed of was how far I had been willing to go to keep him from knowing the truth about me, willing even to give in to Vaughn's evil plan.

Deep down I knew I had to tell Nicholas everything. There was no use trying to justify doing anything else. I had to lay it all before him. Whether he could forgive me, I didn't know.

When Dora came to tell me Nicholas had arrived and was downstairs waiting for me, I had a moment of weakness. Did I really have to risk it all? Risk losing the man I loved? I knew that's what was at stake. How could he love me if he knew my shameful secret?

As I reached the landing of the stairs, I felt faint. I reached out one hand, grasped the newel post to steady myself, and whispered a prayer for the strength to be courageous enough to be truthful.

I might have been Marie Antoinette going to the guillotine as I went down the remaining stairs to Lady Cahill's drawing room. Each step I took led me closer and closer to the inevitable. I imagined Nicholas's anger, his bitterness at my deceit. When I came to the last step, I could see him through the open door to the parlor. He was standing at the fireplace, his back to the hall, looking into the cheerful blaze. He must have sensed my coming or heard my footsteps, for he looked up into the gold-framed mirror above the mantel, and seeing me, his whole face lit up. Smiling, he turned around.

With a few quick strides he crossed the carpet, hands extended to me. "Lyssa, darling."

At his loving tone, I felt my heart clutch painfully. I longed to rush into his embrace, yet I dared not. I tried to speak normally, but my voice sounded tight as I forced it over the hard lump rising in my throat. "Good afternoon, Nicholas."

"Why so formal?" he teased. "We're betrothed, remember? I could at least have a kiss, couldn't I?"

I passed him instead, stepped around the marble-topped table in the center of the room and went to stand behind the curved rosewood sofa.

Nicholas looked puzzled. "What is it, darling?"

He started toward me, but stopped when I held up my hand.

"Nicholas, I have something—something very important—I must discuss with you."

He regarded me with tender amusement. "Of course, darling, but does it have to be discussed at such a great distance? Why don't we sit down together where we can be comfortable?"

From his lighthearted manner, I knew he thought the something important was something trivial, such as some difficulty with the caterers for our reception. Could they provide fresh salmon sandwiches or should the icing on the petit fours be pale green or pink? I wished with all my heart it *was* something so insignificant.

"No, I'd rather not." I shook my head. "Please just listen and don't interrupt." I spoke more rapidly than usual, and I saw both concern and curiosity in Nicholas's eyes.

I slipped off the beautiful lily engagement ring and held it enclosed in my palm. I recalled the symbolism of its design, the pristine pearl, the sparkling diamonds, representing purity and truth, the virtues Nicholas believed I possessed. I didn't deserve to wear it. I would give it back to him before he asked to be released from our engagement. I was convinced that once he knew the truth about me, he would not want me.

But I wanted to hold on to it a little longer, to give me the courage and strength I needed. It represented the pledge of our love and mutual respect, the promise of fidelity. It was a symbol of our belief that from the beginning we were meant for each other and would belong to each other for the rest of our lives.

I gripped the ring as, haltingly, I began my story.

Nicholas listened gravely to all I had to say. I could not tell from his expression what he was thinking or feeling as I stumblingly told him all I'd left out before. How I'd met Vaughn in the Brindles' taproom, agreeing to pose for him in my desperation, of my escape after discovering the stolen goods, the jolt of receiving Vaughn's threatening letter, how I'd planned to pawn my mother's jewels and pay Vaughn the blackmail.

When I came to the part of standing in the crowd watching the stretcher with its tragic burden pass in front of me, seeing the ring, I nearly broke down. But I struggled on to the end. It was the most difficult thing I had ever done.

I could not bear to look at Nicholas to see his reaction. I put my head down, held out the hand with the engagement ring, and opened my palm.

The silence that stretched between us in the room seemed endless. Then I felt Nicholas's hand on mine, felt him pick up the ring from my palm, turn my hand over, and place the ring back on my finger.

I opened my eyes, and slowly he drew me by my hand around from the back of the sofa and into his arms. He smoothed back my hair, and with a sigh that was a half sob, I leaned against him and felt his arms around me. I clung to him, tears running down my cheeks. His lips touched my temples, moved slowly down my cheeks, kissing my tears. I heard such caressing words as "dearest one," "my love." Then his mouth covered mine in a long, tender kiss.

I leaned my head back and looked up at him through tear-blurred eyes. "Oh, Nicholas, you're not disgusted with me or angry? You don't despise me after all I've told you?"

"Challys, my darling, don't you know that nothing you could tell me would change my love for you? I have promised you my heart, my love, my protection—forever. I would never take that back."

Speechless, I gazed at him. "But, Nicholas, how can you accept me after—"

"I love the bravest, loveliest, most truthful person in the

world. I am proud and honored not only to know you but to have you as my wife." He kissed me again.

"The only thing that troubles me," he said then, "is that you have suffered so needlessly. If you'd come to me in the first place, I would have settled it at once without you having to go through all this anguish."

He pulled me again gently into his arms, and a sweet, comforting warmth spread through me.

"Now, listen, my darling, and I hope we never have to discuss this again. It seems Vaughn had a penchant for writing threatening letters, not only to you, but to me and to others as well. A man with that sort of a mind would not bank on simply frightening an innocent young lady.

"He anticipated you might have trouble securing enough money to pay him off. He wrote to me, assuming I would fear a scandal and give in to his demands. He didn't foresee that I would not play his dirty game, that I would take his letter directly to the police, providing them with evidence of his criminal act.

"He also wrote to the Brindles. The information you had given him about the stolen property was a weapon he thought he could use there. He hadn't the sense to know that the Brindles, who were not too bright themselves, were hooked into some clever, experienced thieves and smugglers who would stop at nothing to insure their own safety. I have no doubt they were the ones who did the fellow in.

"The police informed my bank of the blackmail threat. They gave me marked bills to use that could be traced. I then sent the money by messenger to Vaughn at the tavern he frequented, along with the message that I would meet him at his flat to pick up the painting. He never came. In the meantime, he had foolishly flashed his ill-gotten gains in public view, so there were plenty of witnesses who saw he had come into some unexpected cash. The thieves working with the Brindles, already alerted to Vaughn's talkativeness, probably took matters into their own hands and silenced him before the police could catch up with him." .

I looked at Nicholas aghast. "Then, you knew all this!"

"Except that he had threatened you, darling. I had hoped to keep all this unpleasantness from you."

New tears rushed into my eyes. "Oh, Nicholas, let us promise never to have any more secrets between us."

"I agree. If we've learned anything from this experience, it is that trying to keep the truth from someone can hurt rather than help. If we had both told each other the truth from the beginning, we could have prevented the agony caused by Vaughn's threats. The truth would not have endangered our love. Nothing could do that." He pulled me close, so close I could feel his heart pounding against mine. "No more secrets."

After a few seconds in which I enjoyed the lovely security of Nicholas's embrace, I drew back and asked, "But what about the painting?"

Nicholas made a grimace. "Dreadful, my dear! As the newspaper article about him stated, Francis Vaughn was a *sign painter* not an artist, although the poor fellow had grand illusions, or perhaps I should say delusions, about his talent. No wonder his mentor turned the painting down flat. Refused to pay for it. Certainly no one would have recognized *you* as the subject."

"But how do you know? Did you see it?"

"I was notified by the police when his body was recovered. They had found my address in his flat. I went with them to the place." Nicholas shook his head as if to rid himself of the memory.

I recalled Vaughn's secretiveness. "He would never let me see it while he was working on it. What about the Brindles?"

"It seems they and that whole operation had been under surveillance for some time. When I went there myself, shortly after the stagecoach accident in which you and Aunt Isabel were victims, I had my doubts as to whether the Brindle woman was telling the truth. There had been reports of other such mishaps, and it's suspected that some were not accidents at all but were deviously planned. Fallen trees *placed* in the road, perhaps. They'll serve long terms in prison."

Nicholas's arms tightened around me. "To think, my poor darling, you were caught up in that web. From now on, as long as I have anything to do with it, nothing will ever harm you, frighten you, or threaten you again."

My favorite stories as a child had been fairy tales with happy endings, though often over the past years I had doubted such things existed outside of books. Now every wish I had ever dreamed was coming true.

Also in fairy tales, the "dragon" always comes to a deserved end. When Nanny Grace accepted our invitation to come to the wedding and live with us afterward at Briarwood Manor, she came with the news of Muir's demise. Riding home one cold, snowy night from an evening of imbibing at the village pub, his horse slipped on a slick bridge, throwing the inebriated Muir into the rushing stream below. His half-frozen body was found the following morning.

Few could mourn the death of such a cruel rogue. For my brother and me it was the lifting of the shadow that had hovered over us since running away from Crossfields. Gone forever was the possibility that Ty might be taken back by his father. He was safe and happy now, the center of the lives of our elderly relatives, and he was looking forward to the protection and love of Nicholas, once we were wed.

I was never so aware of God's gracious mercy as I was during those happy days prior to my wedding. He had protected me through everything leading up to this moment in my life, through the dangerous valleys and dark places, to bring me safely to the desires of my heart.

Nicholas and I were married in Meadowmead's centuries-old, gray stone church on a December morning newly blanketed with snow. My gown was white satin, trimmed at the rounded neck and wrists with narrow bands of ermine. I wore a veil of antique lace that Lady Bethune had worn as a bride. Mama's sapphire and diamond jewelry caught the light from the flames of the six ivory tapers on the altar as I reached the end of the aisle on Uncle George's arm.

When Nicholas and I said our vows, we exchanged matching rings of twisted gold on which two clasped hands were carved.

Our honeymoon was the reverse of most newly wed couples. Nicholas and I spent ours at Briarwood Manor in the recently renovated, newly furnished wing. Instead of going on a wedding trip ourselves, Nicholas had arranged for Aunt Evelyn and Uncle George to spend the rest of the winter in the warm, sunny climate of Italy, and Ty was to stay at Lady Bethune's for a fortnight. Nicholas's aunt had taken quite a fancy to my little brother, saying he reminded her of Nicholas, her favorite nephew, when he was the same age.

My heart was full of thanksgiving for all my unexpected blessings following the time of trouble and trial.

The early winter dusk cast purple shadows across the snow as Nicholas and I entered our home together. As I turned to look at my new husband, I saw in his eyes the love I had always longed to know.